THE
LOPSIDED
ANGEL

To Parsons Public
Library

Nolan Carlson

THE LOPSIDED ANGEL

Nolan Carlson

Hearth
PUBLISHING
Hillsboro, Kansas

First Printing, 1996
Printed in the United States of America
Produced by Hearth Publishing, Inc., Hillsboro, Kansas

Cover Illustration — Jon Goodell
Cover Design — Denise Brueggeman-Siemens

Publisher's Cataloging in Publication
(Prepared by Quality Books Inc.)

Carlson, Nolan K.
    The lopsided angel / Nolan Carlson.
    p. cm.
    Preassigned LCCN: 96-79034.
    ISBN 1-882420-29-2

    I. Title.
    PS3553.A75L66 1996   813'.54
                            QBI96-40677

To O.F.O.W with affection.

Chapter 1

Carl Wadonelli pulled off his worn work gloves. Opening the tap at the kitchen sink, he ran cold water on his hands, splashed his face, and finally dampened the back of his sunburned neck. Pete, a ten-year-old, mixed-bred mongrel collapsed at his feet, its tongue draping out of the corner of its mouth, panting from the Kansas heat.

"Whew!" Carl said, wiping his face with a towel, "It's going to top 100 again today for sure. Everything is burning up out there. There' s thunderheads forming in the north, though."

"Your lunch is on the table. There's a pitcher of tea in the refrigerator," Joan Wadonelli said in a dry, monotone voice from the livingroom.

Carl glanced over his shoulder. He winced. His wife was in the same chair watching the same inane sitcom which came on at this time every day. "Aren't you coming in to join me, Joan?" he asked, forcing his voice to sound cheerful.

"No. You go ahead. I'm not hungry."

Carl nodded to himself. Picking up a sandwich from the plate, he munched on it looking out the window at the endless rows of corn in the field, crisp and burned. He stared into the wavy heat mirages in the distance, then the concrete silo, the cracked earth below it, and the bicycle tipped on its side near the barn. He turned away as the bread suddenly clogged his throat. Tipping his cap back, he walked toward his wife.

"Here, have a glass of tea," he said.

Joan sipped the tea, transfixed to the antics on the 19 inch black and white T.V. screen. She didn't respond to the canned laughter.

Carl lowered himself into the divan opposite his wife. He saw the laundry heaped in the basket, the vacuum cleaner still in the middle of the room, and the newspapers strewn on the floor. "Drought's burning everything up," he said. "Everything is scorched and dying. Corn crop's about done in. Can't afford to irrigate. We've got a loan payment due next week."

"What?" Joan asked, her eyes glued to the set.

"Nothin'," Carl answered, taking a drink of tea. "You going to your meeting this afternoon? I could drop you off. I've got to go in to pick up a part for the tractor."

Joan glanced toward him but avoided his eyes. "What meeting?"

"Your guild. Don't they meet on the third Thursday of the month?"

"Oh, yes." She turned back to the television. "No, I don't think so. I've got too much to do here at the house."

Leaning forward, Carl traced the frosted glass across his flushed forehead. "It might do you some good. It might take your mind off of it for a little while."

Joan did not reply.

"You can't hide from everyone forever, you know."

Abruptly, Joan rose and snapped off the T.V. with a gesture of impatience. "What are you, a psychologist or something?"

Carl shook his head. "No. But, I can tell when someone is running away from herself."

Joan pulled an article from the clothes basket and carelessly folded it.

"You can't hide in this house forever."

"I'm not hiding. I went to mass Sunday and got groceries on Tuesday."

"Yeah. In and out as fast as you could."

Joan pressed her fingers to her closed eyelids. "I'm trying. Don't criticize." She looked up, her jaw set. "I'm just not ready. I don't want to chat idly at a women's club or talk about the drought. It's all so unimportant compared to..." She ran her bare foot along Pete's back lying at her feet.

2

Carl reached out but hesitated several inches from her shoulder. His eyes were soft with understanding. "I know, hon. But, we've got to go on. It's been over three months now."

"Three months," she said bitterly. "Three months are nothing compared to a lifetime."

Carl leaned back, allowing the breeze from the rotating fan to cool his face.

"If only Ricky hadn't been so adventurous. He was always trying dangerous things," she said.

Carl bit into the inside of his cheek. "He was a little boy, Joan. Eight-year-old boys try things."

"We warned him time and again not to go down to that pond." She shook her head and gazed out the window. "It's hard to believe now how it rained in April. That pond was brimming full. We told him we'd swat his behind good if he went down there." Her voice broke. "I'm so mad at him."

"Ricky loved the water. He would've been a natural swimmer. We were going to have him take lessons in town this summer."

Joan smiled to herself in thought. "Remember that time he made that swing from the rafters. He jumped from the loft and swung the full length of the barn. He could've hung himself. And there was the time, when he was six, that he hid in the bed of the pickup so he could go to town with you. It was just lucky that you discovered it a few miles from home. He could have fallen out of there." She kneaded the back of her neck. "He was always trying something."

"He was quite a kid. A chip off the old block, I'd say. I was always getting into trouble as a kid."

Joan looked away. "Yeah, a chip off the old block. You liked his daredevil trait," she said, accusingly.

"I admired everything about him." Carl sipped his tea thoughtfully. "I can't even get myself to put his bike away for the last time. Rick never put it away like he was supposed to. When you called him in for supper he'd just hop off and let it slam to the ground and he'd come racing to the house his white hair flying." Carl chuckled dryly. "The bike was always there waiting for him in the morning." He looked up. "Remember that willow branch he stuck in the ground in your zinnia bed a few months ago. He just knew it would grow. He was so sure of everything."

"If I told him once, I told him a thousand times to put that bike in the shed when he was through with it. He never listened," she said wearily.

Carl got to his feet and placed a gentle hand on his wife's shoulder. "Joan, honey, maybe there can be another Ricky some-day, God willing."

Joan pulled away, then turned to him with eyes vacant and cold. "Don't talk to me about God, Carl. "There aren't going to be any more kids and we both know it. We've been told by all kinds of doctors that it was almost a miracle that I became pregnant with Ricky. It took years of tests and treatments as it was. Besides, we're not that young any more."

"Joan ... don't torture yourself."

Joan wilted into a large overstuffed chair and stared at the floor. "I'm just a walking, talking, breathing shell," she said solemnly. "Nothing seems worthwhile anymore. Food doesn't taste. I don't feel the wind or smell the fresh cut alfalfa. Sympa-thy from folks leaves me cold. I don't want it or their casseroles and canned preserves."

Tears escaped from Joan's eyes and rolled down her con-torted face. She angrily wiped them away with the back of her hand. "When Ricky stopped living, I did too. In a way, I'm as dead as he is. I'm just going through the motions of a living being. I go to church and sing the glories and praises of God when I really doubt that there is one." She raised her head and her voice grated with bitterness. "If there is a God, a powerful God, a God of mercy and goodness, why would He ever allow something like this to happen?"

Carl bit into his lip. "You know there's no answer, Joan. A small farmer like me sure can't answer it. I just think He lets us live as we live. We make our lives what they are. But I do know we've got to learn to accept our son's death."

"I have accepted it," she said sadly. "A body accepts it when there's no sound of a little boy's wagon squeaking as he pulls it along or when you suddenly don't have to wipe up muddy tracks on the kitchen floor on rainy days, or when you don't feel the warmth of him in your lap when you read a fairy tale ... or hear him repeat his prayers before bed time."

Carl grabbed his wife's arm with urgency. "Stop it, Joan! You're tearing yourself apart. For three months now you've cried yourself to sleep. Yes, Ricky is dead. We're never going to see or hear him again. It's hell, I know. It doesn't seem fair. I don't have a hint of any reason behind it." He shrugged. "But it's all part of a plan too deep and mysterious for mortals to understand, just like Father Shawn said."

Joan's expressionless eyes stared into the pleading eyes of her husband. "God may bring life into the world, Carl, but He also destroys it when it serves no purpose. He killed our son and He's going to send down the vengeance of a drought and kill your crops. He's refused rain these past months to growing things and they will die too."

"What about the lives He's brought into the world?"

"It's better to never have life at all than to smother it out after others have learned to love it as we did Ricky."

Carl backed away from his wife in defeat. He lowered his glass to the table then, without another word, raced out the kitchen door. Pete hurried to catch up with him.

Joan watched the menacing dark clouds rolling through the sky from the livingroom window. She looked down the stone path leading to the graveled country road. Ricky's shrill screams of joy seemed to fill the quiet room in her mind. She smiled to herself seeing him delivering a package from the mail box by the road. One hand tried to control the careening bike while the other clutched the package. The bike wobbled and Ricky laughed, displaying wide gaps of lost teeth.

A large gray cat darted across her line of vision. It's long lean frame was once fat and silken. It now appeared mangy and sick. It crept stealthily from refuge to refuge finally springing into the shadows of the barn. Joan remembered when it used to lie tame and content in Ricky's arms. Now it slinked and cowered like a wild animal.

With stoic eyes, Joan looked at the bare patches of ground where Ricky had built pretend-roads for his toy trucks and cars. Carl disposed of all of Ricky's belongings immediately after the drowning except for the bike still laying out in the yard. He gave everything to thrift shops and the Salvation Army .

But even so, everywhere Joan looked she saw her son laughing, running, and climbing. He was always in perpetual motion. She closed her eyes tightly. How would she ever get over his death? How could she go on living?

Opening her eyes, she stretched to see the pond in the north pasture barely visible above the fields of swaying stalks of corn. It was now just a few shallow circles of stagnant mud. A few months ago, during the many torrential April rains, it had been bank full inviting an adventurous boy in for an early swim.

She mentally retraced that terrible day in her mind for the thousandth time. She remembered flying out the screened door, barefoot, racing toward Carl carrying Ricky's limp body to the house. She remembered looking at him lying at her feet in the grass, pale, his blonde hair matted to his forehead. She had looked up at Carl wanting him to fix him like he always fixed everything from his broken combine to the agitator on her washing machine. But his eyes told her that this time he could do nothing.

Joan recalled turning abruptly and coming back into the house hardly noticing the thick smoke which filled the kitchen from the burned cookies in the oven. Peanut butter — Ricky's favorite. They were to be his mid-afternoon snack.

After that day she hardly left the house except for the funeral. She went to the grocery store once a week, and church on Sundays. Everything once important and meaningful in her life shrank to obscurity. Her half-finished, crocheted table cloth lay in the sewing basket without progress. The ladies' section of the Lawton Sentinel remained unread. Pride in her cooking dwindled and turned into duty and drudgery. She was, as Carl said, merely going through the motions of living.

Her thoughts were pushed aside by Carl's shouts coming from the kitchen. She hadn't heard the slam of the outside screen door.

"Joan, Joan, you in the house?"

Joan continued staring across the field toward the pond that had taken her son's life.

Carl stood in the doorway blinking his eyes trying to adjust them to the darkened room. "Oh, there you are. Looking at the storm brewing, huh? That came up real fast."

She continued staring toward the pond. "The storm doesn't matter to me one way or another."

Carl tried to smile. "How about me putting on the coffee pot? We could have some of Shirley Craven's sweet rolls with it."

Joan shook her head. "I don't want any coffee and I don't want any of Shirley Craven's sweet rolls."

The little frame house vibrated as the wind increased in intensity.

"Wind's getting stronger. The storm's going to reach here shortly." Carl pushed up a hassock and sat down close to his wife. Reaching out, he took her hand and looked into her eyes. "You're remembering, aren't you, Joan? You're remembering that day. You're remembering the way Rick used to romp and play and laugh."

Joan didn't answer.

"I remember him too. I still turn around when I'm milking expecting him to be standing there holding that gray cat begging for some squirts of milk. When I pull that old settin' hen off her nest I can still hear him squeal as he always did when she flapped her wings and squawked like she was being killed." He sighed. "When I go in the pickup for feed, it doesn't seem right not to have him next to me craning his neck to see over the dashboard. I see him hitting the ball I pitch him a country mile.

That kid was a natural. Maybe even big league material some-day. He could do anything. It still seems as though I expect to turn around and see his happy, dirty little face staring up at me … but I don't anymore."

Joan looked down at the bent head of her husband. She saw his body quake and heard a strained gasp exploding from his mouth. It was the only time, except for the funeral, that she had seen him cry. She withdrew her hand from his and touched his wet cheek.

"I've been selfish, Carl. I've been hurting so badly I never real-ized or cared about what you have been going through. All this time you've had to hide your pain and be strong for me." She pulled him easily into her arms and comforted him like a small child. "I'm really ashamed of myself."

Carl finally eased himself from her embrace and wiped his face with his handkerchief. "Sorry, Joan. I had to do it or I think I would have strangled. The hurt was choking me." He looked out the window at the black, gravid clouds racing through the sky. He took a deep breath. "Joan, let's go outside and watch the storm."

Joan reached for his extended hand. Without a word they walked together out into the dark day. A jagged spear of lightning flashed in the north.

The wind whipped Joan's cotton dress about her. She wan-dered about the yard as though she had just returned from a long trip. A chicken scuttled in front of her and she shooed it through the open gate. She always scolded Ricky for leaving the gate open allowing the chickens to enter the yard. She couldn't stand chicken droppings in the yard.

Carl looked up at the clouds, watching them race one another. He picked up a large, broken limb and heaved it from the yard.

Joan stopped a rolling egg bucket with her foot and placed it on the porch. With her arms folded she walked down the stone walk for the first time in three months. She looked down at the sorry remnants of her once flourishing flower bed. The plants now drooped brown and brittle in the baked soil. Her eyes swept down row after row of wilted petunias, periwinkles, and zinnias until they reached the back of the small plot where they widened with disbelief.

Ricky's small willow cutting stood supple and strong swaying in the wind. Several slim, shiny leaves waved in the breeze. Joan walked straight to the little tree. The dried flowers crunched beneath her feet. She knelt before the little tree and felt the tender leaves. Tears crowded the corners of her eyes as she smiled. "He was always so sure of everything," she whispered.

Carl saw his wife kneeling before Ricky's willow sapling. An instant wave of hope shot through him. "It's alive, Joan! It's the only thing alive in the whole darned bed."

Joan pulled away the weeds that had crowded around it. Her voice shook with emotion. "It's more than alive. It's strong and growing."

"You see, Joan, God wanted that little tree to live. He kept a divine eye on it all this time."

"Carl, go get some water for it. We've got to help save it for Ricky's sake ... and for ours."

Carl turned and started for the outdoor faucet.

"And Carl ... "

He stopped in his tracks and turned around.

"What time is it?"

Carl glanced at his watch. "Quarter 'til three."

"You still going in to town to get that part?"

He nodded. "I've got to have it even if it does storm."

"I think I'll ride in with you. You've wanted me to see Father Shawn and I don't want them to vote on that new stove for the parish hall without my say."

Chapter 2

Joan sat rigid in the uncomfortable ornate-back chair. When she leaned against the hard back her feet barely touched the floor. She glanced at the faded flowered wallpaper and took note of the water stain on the ceiling. She looked at the stark room, bare except for the spaced religious icons on the walls. The room was huge and austere. It was obvious to her that it was a man's sanctuary. There was no evidence of feminine intrusion. There were no flowers, no frills. It was purely functional.

"I'm glad you agreed to come and see me, Joan. I've thought about you a lot since the funeral."

Joan looked at the priest. His muscular body and angular features made her think he looked like a prize fighter or something. In fact, she heard that as a young man he did amateur boxing. His ruddy complexion and coarse bright red hair attested to his Irish background. And she noticed an inherited, troublesome cowlick on the back of his head. Two furry caterpillar eyebrows ran across his forehead. He was young as priests go; middle forties. He was ordained twenty years ago in Kansas City. St. Regis was his third parish in that time. She was sure there were priests who grew up in towns of barely a few hundred who spent their entire vocation ministering to city people and priests who grew up in huge cities and spent their entire vocation ministering to a rural population.

Suddenly, Joan noticed that Father Shawn was looking at her expectantly.

"I was in town with Carl and went to a guild meeting when I saw your light on," she stammered.

"I'm glad you stopped by."

"Maybe I came at a bad time. I didn't even call for an appointment."

Father Shawn smiled warmly and shook his head. "You came at exactly the right time. I don't have a thing scheduled. I just got back from seeing Marge Hopkins at Valley View, so I've got plenty of time."

Joan knew that wasn't true. With the shortage of priests the last two decades, she knew Father Shawn was busy from early morning until late at night preparing homilies, ministering to the sick, taking communion to the shut-ins, counseling, presiding over the parish council, teaching catechumens, and running to Havensville twice a week since the priest there died at age seventy-eight and no replacement had been found. But, she appreciated him not making her feel guilty.

Father Shawn leaned forward and clasped his hands together on the top of the old, scarred desk. "Where would you like to start?"

Joan bit into her lower lip. "I don't know. I guess I just needed someone to talk to. Someone outside of the family. Carl has been after me to see you for three months now."

"This is an important first step, Joan. I know it took courage to knock on that door today.

She nodded. "Yes, but now what? What good are words? I've been consoled and pampered to death by everyone in town. I've got enough hams, preserves, and casseroles to last a lifetime." She looked down into her lap wistfully. "People have been very kind. But, there's just so much they can do. There's just so much anyone can do."

"Lawton is a wonderful town. It's full of caring, loving people. The Catholic community is very close."

"But, still ... " She looked away.

"But, still what, Joan?"

"It doesn't seem to matter, Father. I'm still empty and sad ... and bitter. Terribly bitter and angry."

"It's like a fresh wound, Joan. The tragedy is still very raw. It will take time to heal."

12

A bolt of anger shot through her. If this was all he was going to offer, pitiful platitudes, she would walk right out, she thought angrily. During her years of Catholic upbringing she had always been taught to be respectful and reverent to the clergy from her traditional Catholic parents as well as the nuns at St. Agnes' parochial school, but if he was going to just offer positive sayings, she would walk out, by damned, she told herself.

"It's going to take time, Joan. You'll never forget that terrible day as long as you live. Every time Ricky's birthday comes along, the anniversary of his first communion, Christmas, school starting, what would have been his confirmation … "

"Stop it!" She couldn't believe she had spoken that way. Shame waved through her and her face reddened. Mentally, she saw the stern faces of her parents silently reprimanding her. Father Shawn, however, didn't flinch.

"You've got to face all of this, Joan. It will get better for you, but it will never disappear."

"Then," Joan said dryly,"I don't know if I can stand it. I … I don't know if I want to stand it."

"I've heard that quite often during my twenty years as a priest. I've talked with people who've lost children, their parents, their spouse, even their whole family and they all say the same thing. The hurt … the pain … is too much to bear. Some don't want to continue their lives, but almost all of them seem to have this miraculous will, this miraculous reserve of courage and strength and they do survive." He knotted his large hands into balls and waved them in emphasis.

"Maybe they're stronger than I am, Father. Maybe they've got more faith."

Father Shawn shook his head and looked into her eyes. "I don't think so, Joan. I don't think so at all. You and your family have always been strong Christians … strong Catholics."

"And what has it gotten us?" She noticed the hardness in her voice. "When I was growing up, we said the rosary before bedtime for years. We never missed mass even when we were sick or the weather was bad. I went to a parochial school until high school and then I belonged to CYO in the public high school. Dad was a lifelong member of the Knights of Columbus holding the office of Grand Knight two different times, and mom was president of her Catholic Women's Guild. My brothers and sisters and I went to confession every week, we all went to weekly religious education classes, went through first communion, confirmation, did community service, attended every holy day of obligation, and went on Catholic retreats. I married a Catholic and Ricky was baptized a Catholic." She extended her arms. "And what did it get us?"

"Your faith will help you, Joan. Don't give up on it."

"Right now, Father Shawn, it means nothing to me. I'm not even sure there is a God." She noticed the cold shiver that raced down her back after uttering such a blasphemous statement. But Father Shawn remained sober and composed.

"That's not an unusual statement for someone hurting like you are. I've also heard that many times over."

"How could a benevolent, caring God take the life of an innocent child?"

"What makes you think God was responsible for taking your son's life?"

"Isn't He supposed to be the epitome of love and goodness ... and power? He has more power than all of the people on earth put together. Why didn't He use his power to prevent my son's death?"

"God was not responsible for Ricky's death. God allows us our free will. God is as sad as you are that Ricky is gone."

Joan bandied her head about. "I don't know. I just don't understand. I'm so hurt, so empty, so sad, and so mad."

"At God?"

"At God and Ricky as well. Why did he try to swim in that pond? Why was he always so daring? Why did he allow his life to be snuffed out and have all the wonderful years ahead of him disappear? He took away, from Carl and me, years of watching him grow into manhood. He took away our grandchildren and future generations."

"So you're mad at God and Ricky for depriving you of the pleasure of being a part of your son's life."

"Yes! That's it exactly. I keep thinking what could have been." Joan slumped in her chair feeling drained. "Carl and I just miss him so much."

Father Shawn reached out and took her hand. "I know, Joan, I know. God and I both understand your hurt and anger. God has broad shoulders, so if you want to curse Him and revile Him, go ahead. You have His permission and mine."

Joan looked up, her eyes crowded with tears. "You know there can never be any more children for us, don't you, Father?"

"What do you mean?"

"I had a terrible time getting pregnant with Ricky. I had many miscarriages before that. There were all kinds of tests and treatments. When I finally did become pregnant I had to lie flat on my back the last four months before delivery. The doctors said it was a miracle that we ever had him."

"Perhaps God will work another miracle for you and Carl. He's pretty skilled in the miracle department."

Joan pulled her hand from Father Shawn's grasp, wiped her tears, and blew her nose. "I wouldn't plan on it, Father. I think we're only allotted one miracle per lifetime."

"Don't sell God or yourself short, Joan."

Joan looked away, concentrating on a small pewter crucifix on his desk.

"You could at least get a couple of doctors' opinions. There still might be hope."

Joan shook her head. "Not at this point. It's futile. Besides, Carl and I are in our forties now. It would be more difficult than ever."

Father Shawn leaned back and clasped his hands behind his head in thought. His eyes gazed at the ceiling as though he were waiting for divine guidance. Suddenly, he bounded forward and looked intently at Joan. "Have you ever thought about being foster parents or adoption? I know there's a big demand for foster parents in this county. And I think Catholic Charities in

Stockton might have some kids that are open for adoption or foster care."

Joan looked up. "There are babies out there to adopt?"

"You might consider one or the other; adoption or foster parenting."

Joan shrugged. "I don't know. I don't know if we're ready for anything like that. It's too soon. It wouldn't be respectful to Ricky."

Father Shawn nodded. "Of course. It was only a thought." He pulled his desk drawer open and it squealed in protest. He brushed aside articles and fished beneath papers and a menagerie of items. "Here it is," he said at last, a satisfied grin on his face. He extended his hand holding a smudged, wrinkled business card.

"What's that?"

"Sister Angelica's card at St. Vincents in Stockton. She's director of Catholic Charities."

Joan's brow wrinkled quizzically.

"Just in case you decide some day to look into it. I mean, if there is absolutely no hope of ever having your own. There are children out there who would be very grateful for the home and family you and Carl could provide."

Joan took the card and dropped it uncaringly into her purse. "Thank you, but I don't think we'd ever be interested. If we can never have any of our own, we just will never have any, that's all."

"I understand. It was just a thought," Father Shawn said pushing the drawer closed. He sighed. "And now let me find you some scripture to give you some comfort."

He flicked through the Bible and paused at various places marked for certain occasions. "Read John, Chapter 11, about Jesus' resurrecting Lazarus. It shows the mercy and power of God." He searched some more. "And perhaps read the prayer of understanding in Psalms, Chapter 119 verses 33-40 and also the prayer for help in Psalms, Chapter 130 verses 1 through 8." He continued to search through the pages. "And then ... "

"That will probably be enough for now, Father," Joan said

impatiently. She looked at her watch. "I really need to go. Carl is waiting in the truck."

Father Shawn nodded. "Of course." He handed her the Bible. "Use my Bible for a time. There are dog ears and markers for the places I think will help you."

Reluctantly, Joan took the Bible.

"You can return it to me on your next visit."

Joan nodded, realizing she was not at all sure there would be a second visit. "Thank you, Father. I appreciate your kindness and help."

"Would you like to schedule another appointment today?" He reached for his appointment calendar. "Next Tuesday evening looks free."

Joan lowered her eyes. "I don't know just now. Maybe I could call later in the week."

Father Shawn nodded. "Yes, that would be fine. You check your schedule with Carl and let me know. If Tuesday doesn't work for you, I'm sure I can shuffle some things around."

Getting up abruptly, clutching the Bible a bit too intently, Joan pushed her chair back. The strident sound of the legs on the bare wood floor caused her to lurch. "Yes, I'll do that." She turned and walked briskly to the door.

"You will read those passages, won't you, Joan? And you will consider returning?"

She could feel his piercing blue eyes knife through her as though he were reading her intentions.

"I ... I will, Father. And thank you again." She hurriedly walked through the doorway to the main door of the rectory.

"May God be with you, Joan," Father Shawn called out as the door crashed closed.

Joan failed to hear him as she was already on the porch and scurrying down the steps.

Chapter 3

A dense cloud of smoke settled over the green, felt-covered table. The stench and smoke of many cheap cigars, cigarettes and pipes represented concentration, satisfaction, and frustration. One or two of the men took abbreviated puffs, letting the smoke out in spurts from between clenched teeth. Those were the concentrators. One or two others drew in long, deep, calm puffs that moved the ash along rapidly. They were the satisfied, reveling in the comfort of their good hand for the moment. The frustrated and angry took short puffs laying their cigars aside checking the eyes of their opponents before starting to smoke again.

The monthly poker game was at Charley Nelson's house. His wife and kids were out of town visiting her mother. This was a bit of convenient luck as each of the other players made excuses to disallow them from having the game at his house. The men were pleased. Even the ones losing were content. This was masculine domain. There was no "lady of the house" peeking around the corner with raised eyebrows nodding to her spouse and tapping on her watch crystal bringing the game to an abrupt close.

The men lined their beer bottles up like a company of well-drilled soldiers. They wore caps and faded teeshirts. Their top pants' buttons were opened. The host provided two pounds of liverwurst, a log of cracker barrel cheese, and a box of Ritz crackers on one corner of the table for his guests.

Carl was five dollars behind, but he felt good anyway. He had needed this night out for a long time. This was his first time out since Ricky's death. He pulled his cigar from his mouth and brought up a deep, hollow belch. All of these guys were his friends. They were all third degree Knights of Columbus members, Council 1790. He liked each and every one of them.

Ollie Culver leaned back on the legs of the kitchen chair and sucked his cigar in contemplation. "Bet a dime." He tossed in a red chip.

Kebert Thomas cocked his brow and threw in his chip. "I'm staying with you. I'll call."

Ollie grinned and put his protruding teeth on full display. "That's what the game is all about. You pay to stay and pray you don't have to pay."

Carl stared at his cards. He felt light-headed after drinking three beers. The game stalled, waiting for him to decide. Ollie moved his tongue over his teeth with impatience.

"Stay or fold," Ollie demanded.

Carl screwed up his face with annoyance. "Listen, I've sunk over two bucks in this pot. I'm just deciding whether it's a good enough risk to call or get out now before I go in deeper. I don't know what you're so hell-fire in a hurry about anyway."

"Hold it, Carl. This isn't getting us anywhere. Are you going to stay or are you getting out?" Kebert asked.

Carl looked up with a frown and slapped his cards on the table. "Out!" he said.

Charley called for a break and replenished everyone's drink. Smokers emptied their ashtrays and a line formed at the bathroom.

Ollie worked away at a cheese and cracker looking much like a beaver gnawing on a tree. "So you're batchin', huh, Charley?" he asked.

Charley paused for a moment after pulling caps off of bottles. "That I am and let me tell you after sixteen years, it's pure joy. No kids yelling and no wife nagging. I come home after working in the field, take off my overalls and just let them drop to the floor. I get me a beer from the refrigerator, make a baloney and onion sandwich, prop my feet up, and sit around in my underwear watching sports." He sighed. "That's what I call living. It doesn't get any better than that."

Kebert set his bottle down. "What I like about batching once in awhile is the informality of it all. Nothing has to be done on schedule. You can let the dishes stack in the sink, let your shoes clutter the rug, and bring your dog in beside you on the couch." He raised his eyes to the ceiling. "But, I do miss Gary if he's gone too long, though." He smiled proudly. "He's quite a kid. A real boy in every sense of the word. Just like Tom Sawyer … always getting into trouble." He smiled in reflection. "Take last week; he pulled up my wife's begonia bed. Pulled them up roots and all and carried them into the house as proud as punch. I thought Betty was going to explode. I nearly laughed myself silly." Kebert looked above the group in reminiscence. "Yeah, kids are a lot of trouble but they're worth it. Life would be pretty dull without them."

Dusty Morton banged his fist on the table. Bottles swayed and hit together and the box of crackers toppled to the floor. "Horse manure! I've been a bachelor for 43 years and I don't regret one day of it. No wife scuffing around in old bedroom slippers and curlers, crabbing and crying about bills, the broken screen door, chickweed in the lawn, and a dozen other things."

Carl tipped his cap back and batted his eyes to clear his head. "Nice talk, Dusty. Real nice talk. You know all of us are married here except you … and happily I might add."

"Right!" everyone said in unison.

"Horse manure!" Dusty reiterated. "Charley and Kebert just got through telling us how great it was to get their wives out of the way awhile so they could prop their feet up and sit around in their underwear."

Leonard Kopple stood up and glowered down at Dusty. "Now, Morton, don't be disrespectful to the weaker sex."

"Weaker sex, right," sneered Dusty. "Women are stronger than water buffalo, each and every one of them. They'd make better construction workers, coal miners, and bridge builders than any man. Statistics show they outlive men by seven years and they've got hearts like jackhammers." He extended his arms in emphasis. "Why, just the act of having a kid … the pain would kill the average man. But a female bounces back to have another in nine months."

Ollie nodded in agreement. "I know it'd kill me to have a kid."

Carl choked and beer sprayed from his bulging mouth.

Big, bashful Leonard Kopple looked over his wire-framed glasses at Ollie. He never cared for these conversations. It was his contention that they were here for cards and they should stay with cards or call it quits. "Come on," he urged. "Let's get back to the game so I can get my six bucks back. Enough of this stuff. I'm ready for more poker."

"Hold on, Lennie. Dusty thinks he's an expert on marriage and kids. Naturally he would, beings he's never been married or had a kid. Those are always the kind who know it all," Ollie retaliated. "Just like the ones who write books on farming and live in New York City."

Dusty smoothed his anemic mustache and cocked his head to one side. "Everyone should know that it is true that an outsider who has nothing to do with a particular thing has a better pro ... per ... perspective of a situation. That's just common knowledge."

"Oh, really?" Carl said, chugging his beer, "Then Dusty, I guess you'd like one of us farmers to give you advice on how to run your hardware store?"

Charley shook his head. " I agree. But in this case I don't think that follows ... no, sir. You've got to be on the inside really to know about marriage and kids. Take kids for instance; you've got to live with them on a day-to-day basis to really know them. A kid is a unique little being." Charley smiled to himself. "No, you've got to be there ... right there when they learn to ride that first bike or discover the beauty of nature, or when they give you a big hug just because they love you and you're their dad. I know I grumble and gripe about them at times, but a kid is a pretty great thing. It's too bad they ever have to grow up."

"Hold on there, Charley," Kebert said. "I love kids but I wouldn't go as far as to say I never would want them to grow up. They're great, but it'll be great to see them strike out on their own, making their way just as we had to years ago." He leaned back in his chair and smiled. "The thing that is wonderful is when they accomplish something really significant in life and you can feel that you had a part in getting them there." He folded his hands on the back of his head and propped his feet up on a chair. "Yeah, they're pretty wonderful. Sometimes they get on your nerves until you feel you're going crazy, but after they're out of the house a while, you miss the noise."

"Bull manure!" scoffed Dusty as he lit a cigar.

"Let's play cards. Isn't that what we came for? You guys sit around and cackle about kids and stuff like a bunch of old ladies." He looked around. "Whose deal is it?" Leonard asked.

Ollie threw the deck in front of Leonard. "It's your deal, Lennie. I don't know how you can just sit there without defending your family. You with four kids and one on the way."

"I just know I don't want anything to do with marriage and kids. I'm what you call a free spirit," said Dusty, expelling a stream of smoke from his nostrils.

"That isn't what I'd call you," Ollie brazenly added with a wry smile.

"You mean somethin' by that, sparrow legs?"

Finally, Carl put his hand up for silence. "Nice talk, you guys ... nice talk. You're all going around in circles and not proving anything. If Dusty wants to stay single, all well and good. Who are we to judge? If we, on the other hand, want to get married and have kids, that's okay too. You know the old saying that a married guy just can't stand to see a friend of his stay single. He won't rest until he gets him married."

"What he's trying to say, is that misery loves company," Dusty added.

Kebert shook his head with vigor. "That isn't true. That isn't true at all. I could care less if you would spend the rest of your life alone and 'free' as you call it. What gripes me is that you try to make out that we're all suckers because we're married and have kids. Wait 'till you get old and you haven't got any kids or grandkids to come see you. You'll regret it then. I got them for insurance against loneliness in my old age. What are you going to have then, Dusty?"

"I'll still have my cronies and I can date all I want. So, don't feel too sorry for me," Dusty answered. "I know you jakes like your wives and kids and everything. I accept all of that stuff. Just don't ram it down my throat."

Suddenly, Leonard looked up at Carl and his face flushed. "I think we've all been pretty insensitive here tonight, fellas."

Every head turned and stared at Carl. Carl hunched his shoulders. "Ah, I know you guys didn't mean anything by it." He felt himself become stone-sober.

"No," Ollie said, shaking his head, "Lennie is right. We should have thought before we opened our big mouths. It hasn't been all that long for you and Joan."

Carl shook his head. "She's not doing too good. She's trying. In fact, she went to see Father Shawn last week. But, it'll take time. Rick was quite a kid, you know."

Everyone nodded in silence.

"He was one of the best, Carl. That kid would have been a natural athlete. He could hit that ball a country mile already in the cookie league. Yes, sir, he was quite a boy," Charley said, nodding his head.

Carl suddenly wanted to get away. He looked around at his friends and saw the sorrow and pity on their faces. He felt his throat constrict and the tears start to well in his eyes. He threw his cards aside. "I'd better go. I shouldn't leave Joan alone this long. I don't know what I was thinking." He checked his watch. It was only 10:30. The games generally lasted until the early morning hours.

"We understand," Ollie said. "Let's all call it a night. In fact, I've got to get up early tomorrow myself."

The rest of the group mumbled their agreement and started counting their chips.

Carl bounded to his feet, his hands balled into tight fists. "No! You guys go ahead. Life can't stop because we lost our boy. You guys go ahead and play." He turned and headed for the door. He looked over his shoulder. "Thanks, Charley, maybe in a couple months I can have it at my house."

Before anyone could answer, Carl bolted out the door and headed for his pickup. He felt hot tears trailing down his cheeks. He swiped them away with anger and blew his nose.

24

Carl's vision blurred as he drove his old GMC pickup recklessly down the graveled road. Rocks hit noisily beneath the vehicle and against the doors and fenders.

His foot pressed carelessly on the gas pedal. In a daze he watched the speedometer needle move steadily upward ... 50 ... 60 ... 65 ...

The truck bounced into large ruts and pot holes. Moonlit stone fence posts and trees lining the road streaked by.

A rock flew up and ricocheted off the windshield leaving a spider-webbed pattern of cracked glass. His head involuntarily flew back.

Carl bit the inside of his cheek. His lower lip quivered as hot tears rushed from his eyes and trailed down his cheeks. There was a strange mixture of emotions trapped within him. He felt anger, sadness, despair, but most of all an aching loneliness and longing for the sight, smell, and feel of his son.

Flashes of memories exploded in his mind: Ricky's white hair flying in the wind as he rode his Western Flyer bike, Ricky's broad smile with the many vacancies where teeth had been after blowing out the eight candles on his last birthday, Ricky playing in the backyard with his toy trucks and cars making engine sounds as he maneuvered them through tunnels and along miniature dirt highways, the look of determination on his dirt-smudged face as he prepared to slug a pitched ball, the look of contentment and compassion on his face as he sat holding his gray cat, running his hand along its silken coat, giggling as he wrestled with Pete on the rug in the livingroom.

And then another moment of memory flashed in Carl's brain. He winced: Ricky lying peacefully in his white casket at the rosary three months ago, dressed in a suit and tie that he reserved for mass on Sunday only. His hair oiled and combed and a conspicuous absence of dirt smudges on his face.

It had been all that Carl could do to keep himself from rushing forward and grabbing his son out of the casket and rushing out the door. No! There was no way in hell that anyone was going to put his precious son, the light of his life, in the ground. There was no way they were going to keep him from touching or seeing him again once the casket lid was closed.

But, he knew he had to be there, strong and brave, to comfort and support Joan even though she appeared dazed and disoriented after the shot Doc Anderson gave her two hours before the rosary started.

As they moved from one decade to another he could hear the shrieks and wails of his grandmother Wadonelli who vented her emotions and grief to the extreme just like an old-country Italian lady should. He knew the local folks were sad and heartbroken, but they were people from small towns who were reserved and who kept their emotions in check as a rule. He noticed surreptitious glances in grandmother Wadonelli's direction from time to time as her shrill cries seemed to vibrate the stained glass windows of the chapel. She and his sister and brother-in-law and their five kids came from Kansas City that morning. Carl's mother and father were deceased, killed in an auto accident thirty years ago. He and his sister Leona May went to live with grandma Wadonelli in the city when he was ten years old. He knew right away that wasn't where he belonged. Even though he loved her and even though he calmly put up with her histrionics and dramatics he still knew that he was and always would be a farmer just like his father was. As soon as he was able, he left and took over the family farm which had been rented out since his parents' deaths. Mama, as she was called by all who knew her whether kin or not, knew she would never be a farm woman. She had lived in Naples in the old country and she would live in the city in this country. With a monumental show of emotion, she bade him farewell that day many years ago.

Carl loved them all but remembered breathing a sigh of relief when they loaded up in their 1968 Pontiac Chieftain and headed back to the city after the funeral the next day. Mama's cries could be heard two blocks away coming from the open window of the car.

Carl's truck, now clocking 70 miles per hour, suddenly skidded as the passenger side wheels dipped into the edge of the culvert. Carl pulled the wheel sharply to the left with a grunt, just in time to save it from catapulting into a nearby ravine.

Sweat beaded on his forehead. His heart pounded in his chest, but he noticed that he strangely felt no fear. He knew that he was now at the stage of allowing whatever happened to happen. His death, he told himself, would be a coward's way out. The ache and longing would be over. The gut-wrenching sorrow would finally end. But, who would look after Joan? he asked himself.

Carl's thoughts swept back to the poker game tonight. He replayed the conversations of his friends doting on their kids, except for Dusty of course, who was a perennial bachelor. He saw the pride and joy in their faces as they talked about their kids' achievements and disarming mischief. And then, when it occurred to them that they were being thoughtless, he remembered the look of sympathy and pity on their faces. They stumbled over their words of apology and regret each of them telling him of their admiration of Ricky.

"The kid was a natural." "He did everything well." "He was one in a million." Carl and Joan had heard so much praise of Ricky from others over the past three months. They knew he was special. Even his birth had been extraordinary, a miracle. He was smart, athletic, and all boy from the top of his towhead to the bottom of his sneakered feet.

Suddenly, Carl's truck plummeted into a rocky, washed out section at the edge of the road. The cab nosed downward and then vaulted up. A quick glance at the speedometer showed the vehicle traveling at 75 miles per hour. Carl gripped the wheel as the truck rocked dangerously back and forth. The brakes squealed and the smell of burned rubber flooded through the open side windows. It bucked and weaved for a quarter of a mile. At last it shot off the road, rammed through a barbed wire fence and careened up an embankment finally coming to rest on an incline. The motor sputtered and died and everything was eerily silent except for the distant bawling of frightened cattle and the creak of contracting metal.

Carl stared ahead watching the flood of insects circle the head-lights. He sat listening to the thud of his racing heart. His hands still clenched the steering wheel. Burned rubber stung his nostrils.

And then he saw it. It was ethereal in its appearance. It was only half-way materialized. At first he could see the background scenery through it but it seemed to solidify as it got closer. It floated in slow motion progressing closer and closer to the truck through the twin beams of light.

Carl moved forward in his seat straining to see. And then he smiled. It seemed quite natural to him. It was Ricky running toward him with a big smile on his face which displayed the many gaps due to the missing teeth. He wore a striped polo shirt, patched jeans, sneakers, and his old baseball cap with the New York Yankee logo. Carl noticed his eyes. They were dancing with excitement. In his right hand, Ricky carried his favorite Ted Williams' bat. His mouth was wide open and he appeared to be shouting, but Carl heard no sound.

"Rick ... son ... ," Carl said in a mesmerized whisper. "Come here, son," he repeated.

And then Ricky or the vision or whatever it was disappeared in the glare of the truck lights. Carl searched frantically for it.

He bumped open the truck door with his shoulder. The momentum caused him to fall to the ground. The scent of newly mown alfalfa and wild flowers were in the air. The moon was full, casting a pale glow upon him.

"Rick!" he shouted. "Where are you, son? Stop playing games." He rushed back and forth searching and shouting like a crazed man. "Let me pitch you a few, Rick. Come back, son!"

At last, Carl stopped and crumpled helplessly in the field. Burrs and thorns dug at him, but he felt nothing. He lay there sobbing, beating the ground in sorrow and desperation for several seconds. Finally, exhausted, his hands bleeding and raw, he went limp. His tear-stained face looked up at the moon ... to the Heavens.

"Please, God," he uttered in a broken, hoarse voice, "help us. Please, help us."

Chapter 4

Mama waddled about in the small apartment trying to make her guests feel comfortable. She pulled at the corners of her shawl. It was early fall and stifling in the apartment but she still had the shawl covering her round shoulders. Her Mama always wore a shawl, so she would always wear a shawl.

Mama fanned her flushed face with a lace hanky and then wiped between her second and third chins. Even though she was over eighty, her hair was still jet black and reflected the light. Tonight, she wore her black silk with a nosegay of red cloth roses pinned between her ponderous breasts. She gestured at every word whether Italian or English. She spoke English but slipped conveniently back into Italian whenever there was something she did not want Carl's nephews and nieces to understand. Herbert, Carl's brother-in-law and Joan looked just as puzzled as the children while Leona May (Carl's sister) and he smiled and nodded with comprehension. Both of them understood Italian, but neither could speak it.

Mama now lived alone since Papa had died thirteen years ago. She had vowed on Papa's soul never to look at another man, let alone marry again.

When Papa Wadonelli was buried, she draped her large body over the coffin, wailing hysterically refusing to allow it to be lowered into the ground. Mama was a very emotional woman and proud of it. If a woman didn't scream, cry, and tear at herself at a wake, she wasn't worth her salt, in Mama's eyes. She once went to a wake and moaned, groaned, bawled, and squealed finally swooning out of her chair only to be lifted by three heaving men to a little cot in the back room of the mortuary. There she wailed and keened her grief during the entire rosary. She was finally helped out to the car supported by two bullnecked Italians, both groaning beneath her weight. Mama cried out the deceased's name over and over again with shrill, desperate shrieks only to be finally corrected. Her third cousin on her Aunt Maria's side was named Giovanni, not Pietro.

Mama loved wakes, baptisms, funerals, and weddings. They all allowed the right to clutch one's relatives in a fervor of sorrow and happiness. They also allowed for a sumptuous buffet later when the relatives got together. But, the only times her cries of emotion were genuine and directly from the heart, was at the rosaries of her beloved husband, her son and daughter-in-law (Carl's parents), and when Ricky died. For these funerals, she even lost her appetite.

Mama dipped her finger into the spaghetti sauce and tasted it and then licked her upper lip with satisfaction. She pulled at her goading corset. With deft, sure strokes she cut generous chunks of garlic bread and heaped them, smoking, on a platter. She refused to allow Joan or Leona May to help her. Afterall, they were the guests.

Carl and Joan sat opposite Leona May and Herbert in a sway-back, horsehair couch adorned with crocheted doilies on the arms. Immaculata, Mama's cat, peeked out from beneath the couch watching for signs of the children. It had been five months since Ricky's funeral and finally after many written invitations and phone calls Joan relented and agreed to accompany Carl to Kansas City for a Sunday dinner with Mama and Carl's sister, brother-in-law and their five out-of-control children. Already, she could feel a headache making its way from the base of her skull to her crown.

From the dining room, Mama waved at flies with a dish towel. "Why did our Lord ever make these pesky creatures?" She folded her hands and lowered her head for a moment. "And why does Mama know more than the Creator? Mama forgets her place, sometimes," she said quietly as she re-adjusted her shawl.

Lonnie Frank, age eleven and the oldest of the brood, sat quietly in the corner unraveling his sock. The thread was already three yards long and his sock was fast disappearing. Edith Ann, age six, was picking her nose and Herbie Jr., age seven, was dipping his hand in the fish bowl trying to snare a darting fish. Little Joey, age eight, was standing on a chair trying to reach an antique candy dish filled with peppermints. Donna Marie, the youngest at eleven months, was toddling around, her diapers around her ankles.

Mama screamed to Leona May. "Leona May, come in here! Your Lonnie Frank has got his sock almost gone. Herbie Jr. just stepped on my prize guppy and Little Edith Ann has her finger up her nose clear to the knuckle!"

Just then the candy dish fell from the old hutch brought over from the old country, and crashed to the floor spraying mints and broken glass throughout the room.

Mama screeched in horror at the sound of her grandmother's candy dish broken into slivers. "Good Jesus, give me courage and strength!" She looked up. "Grandma, looking down from Heaven, forgive us all." She turned toward the livingroom. "Leona May! Get in here before I kill me a pack of half-Italians." Mama raised her hands above her head in desperation and then rattled off an Italian prayer of forgiveness.

Leona May, agile for such a stout woman, rounded the corner and with precision, grabbed Lonnie Frank by the collar, batted Edith Ann's finger out of her nose and nudged Herbie Jr. in the posterior. "You children," she screamed, "look what you've done in here. I rest myself for a few minutes and you're causing havoc! Goddarn you kids! I'm ready to go to pieces!"

Mama gasped and covered her ears. "Leona May, stop using our Lord's name in vain! The Lord who gave you breath. The Lord who gave you these children. Papa and I," she looked reverently above her, "never allowed such talk. I'm sure your father and mother, God rest their souls, didn't either."

"I'm sorry, Mama, but these kids drive me crazy sometimes."

Joan picked up Little Joey and placed him on a chair while she swept up the broken bowl.

"Thank you, Joan," Mama said, fanning her face. "It was Grandma Patroni's favorite bowl. It was her pride and joy in the old country." Mama wilted into a chair and fanned her perspiring face. "That gave me a start. I had palpitations for awhile. I thought I was about to join Papa in God's kingdom."

"Mama," Leona May said, "are you about ready to eat? I think the kids are starved. If they were eating, I could keep track of all of them."

"Yes, I'm ready. Go tell your husband and Carl to come and eat."

Carl and Herbie came through the double doors to the dining room, both of their faces flushed. The wine Herbie had brought was showing its effect. Herbie was whispering an off-color joke to Carl.

"'... and then', she said, 'what did you expect?'"

Both men turned beet-red and snorted with muffled hilarity.

Mama gave both men a vicious stare. "Leona May, tell your husband I don't allow dirty talk in this house. Papa never allowed it and the same thing goes for me now that he is gone."

Mama never addressed Herbie in first person since the day Leona May introduced him and she discovered that he was not affiliated with any church and was a truck driver. She made Leona May promise, on Papa's grave, to raise the children Catholic. She prayed each night that he would one day "see the light". After twelve years, and five children, the light still seemed to be hidden from Herbie.

Leona May shot Herbie a reproachful look. "Mama's right, Herbie. For shame your dirty tongue."

Herbie cringed and mumbled his apologies. Carl shook his head and smiled.

"Now, all you starving people. Sit down at Mama's table." With a wave of her hand, everyone scattered to chairs.

Lonnie Frank reached for a hunk of garlic bread and was smartly slapped on the hand by his mother.

Mama made the sign of the cross, folded her hands, and closed her eyes. "Dear Jesus, we thank you for this abundance.

We have gathered here tonight to eat a little spaget and a little bread in harmony. We also thank you, Jesus, and Your Mother, Mary, for watching over us. Please allow Papa to smile down on us tonight. How happy Papa must be under Your care walking those golden streets ..."

Lonnie Frank started to reach for a piece of bread at the pause and was slapped once again.

Mama paused for a moment, her eyes still closed. Joan smiled as she saw Little Joey sneak a piece of bread and cram it into his mouth.

"Forgive the little children, Jesus," Mama continued, "for they let their appetites overcome their reverence. Forgive all of those who still have not discovered You."

Herbie shifted uneasily on his chair.

Mama paused once again. "Bless us all as we break bread together."

"Ma, I'm hungry. When is she goin' to finish?" Leona May kicked Herbie Jr. in the shins. He yipped with a sharp whine.

Joan bit into her lower lip to stifle a giggle.

"... and may You always watch over us throughout our brief time here on Your earth. In our Father's holy name, Amen."

Everyone but Herbie made the sign of the cross. Mama pulled her shawl about her shoulders.

"Come on, come on, all of you. Eat Mama's food. Mama wants everyone to eat their fill. Leona May, tell your husband to eat Mama's spaget. Carl ... Joan ... eat up ... eat up! Children, eat up ... eat up! Pass the food around!"

Dishes clattered together as everyone started to eat.

Carl ladled a hefty portion of spaghetti onto his plate. He then dumped a generous helping of sauce over it. The sauce was thick with large chunks of peppers and onions. It was Mama's secret recipe and had been simmering for hours the night before. She could be staked naked out in the desert over a killer ant hill before she would divulge that recipe.

Mama chattered happily in Italian, her arms flying with exaggerated gestures.

Lonnie Frank, at the other end of the table, draped one strand of spaghetti after another on Edith Ann's head.

Joan looked at Carl and nodded toward the scene.

Herbie was attempting to wind the spaghetti around his revolving fork. Mama stopped and watched Herbie's futile attempts as the spaghetti kept slipping off the fork before arriving at his mouth. Mama pulled a hanky from under her tight sleeve and wiped her perspiring upper lip. She continued her vigil, finally crossing herself for what she was thinking.

"Leona May, in all these years you have still not taught that husband of yours how to eat spaget at my house. What is it, Leona May? Is he beyond teaching? "

Herbie aimed his fork at Mama and started to speak. He looked into her puffy face with the three chins and the small half-closed pig eyes and closed his mouth.

"Isn't it bad enough he is not Italian, doesn't go to any church, and drives a truck?" Mama started to berate Herbie further, but caught Lonnie Frank's creation out of the corner of her eye.

Edith Ann looked out soberly beneath the veil of limp strands of spaghetti. Mama's arms flew toward Heaven beckoning strength as she rattled off a list of saints to come to her aid. "Dear God of all creation, look what that boy is doing to that defenseless child!"

Edith Ann smiled a toothless smile pleased with all the attention she was suddenly receiving.

Leona May bolted out of her seat and grabbed Lonnie Frank's arm. "Give me strength! You little cuss; you're going to drive me crazy!" She glanced at Herbie still sitting there frozen and still pointing his fork at Mama but watching his wife wrench Lonnie Frank's arm.

"Herbie!" Leona May shouted. "Help me with these kids, will you?"

Mama shook her head and looked above her.

Leona May looked at Carl and then to Joan. "Do you see how far they go any more without a father at home to discipline? I'm mother and father. I spank and praise. I wash dirty diapers and wipe runny noses." She raised her hands and gestured. "I'm everything to these kids. A woman can do only so much. I was talking just the other night, and mentioned Daddy to Herbie Jr. A perplexed expression came to his little face as though he didn't know who I meant." She looked toward Herbie Jr. who had both hands in his plate of spaghetti kneading it like mudpies. "Poor little tyke." Leona May then returned to Edith Ann's dilemma. She proceeded to pluck one strand of spaghetti off of her head at a time. She looked at Herbie, forcing her lower lip to tremble. "I can't do it alone, Herbie. I'm only human. I've got five young ones here who need a daddy."

Herbie shifted his skinny frame about in his chair, his face crimson with embarrassment. He mumbled something beneath his breath about "havin' to make a livin'."

"Havin' to make a livin'!" Leona May retorted angrily. "Other men find jobs at home so they can watch after their families."

"What do you expect from that husband of yours, Leona May?" offered Mama.

Joan wiped Edith Ann's head with a paper napkin.

"Now … now, you look, Leona May," Herbie said meekly, "I don't want to air our dirty linen here in front of your relatives this way. A man has to do what he knows best. I'm a good eighteen wheeler. I don't know anything else."

"A good husband and father would find work close to his family. Your Papa was here with me and the children every night. The only night he never slept at my side was the day he died. He never roamed around the country. He stayed near my side to help me raise my family." Mama pushed her huge bosom forward with pride.

Carl sat back in his chair having suddenly lost his appetite. His support was with Herbie. He knew how hard it was to make a living for a wife and five kids.

Joan moved the salad around on her plate with a fork detached from her surroundings. Her forehead started to pulsate. It was a familiar malady she always acquired when she visited Mama.

"Now, you take Carl, for instance. He's a farmer. He stays home and provides for his wife and son ..." Mama paled and clamped her napkin over her mouth. Her eyes flooded with sudden tears.

Joan raised her head and looked at Carl. He glanced down at the table to avoid her eyes.

Leona May's mouth flew open. For once she was speechless.

Everything was totally quiet except for Little Joey hitting his spoon against his plate. Edith Ann looked from one adult to the other puzzled at the sudden silence.

Mama reached out and pulled Joan to her. Her body vibrated with sorrow.

"It's okay, Mama, it's okay," Joan said quietly, trying to comfort her.

Mama released her as tears rushed down her cheeks. "I could pull out my tongue. Papa must be terribly angry at me from Heaven. It came out before I thought."

"It's alright, Mama. It's alright," Carl said trying to console her. "It hasn't been that long. We still look around expecting to see him every day."

Leona May pressed Carl's hand and wiped away her tears. Herbie stared down at the table without saying a word.

"What an angel he was," Mama said, choking. "I know he's Jesus' special angel in Heaven. Anyone so perfect would have to be. Those beautiful blue eyes ... that perfect, angelic face." She looked at Joan. "He reminded me of the Gerber baby food baby when he was an infant. And so smart! That boy knew everything. What a loss it was when that precious child left this earth."

Joan's throat constricted but she managed a small smile. "Please don't feel bad ... any of you. Time is making it a little easier each day."

Carl looked over at his wife and smiled affectionately. "We'll make it. That's the way Rick would have wanted it."

Mama nodded and blew her nose with a loud honk. Finally, she looked up. "Please, eat! Pass the spaghetti!"

Leona May, now composed, threw up her hands. "Mama ...

you wait. I've been sitting here letting you run on and on about Herbie as you always have since the day I married him." Leona May pointed her finger at a wilting Herbie.

Herbie had the look and feel of a rag being pulled and jerked at by two pitbulls. "Yes, my Herbie is on the road and he does leave us often, but he provides, Mama."

Mama glanced at Herbie. "That husband of yours, Leona May; how can you defend him? Praise Jesus that your Papa died before he knew that you married a man who does not stay home with his family." She nodded her head toward Herbie.

Herbie wormed about in his seat.

Joan sat back and watched as she spooned portions of pasta into Donna Marie's open mouth.

Herbie cleared his throat and wiped his mouth on a napkin. Red sauce still encircled his lips. "Mama Wadonelli?"

Mama blinked her eyes in feigned consternation. "Leona May, did I hear something? Did that man of yours say something? In all of these years, that husband of yours has never spoken directly to me. Me ... .the grandmama of his wife. The great-grandmama of his children. Bless God ... he has a voice and a tongue."

Herbie's face flushed with sudden rage. "Will you shutup for a minute!"

Joan turned and smiled and cautioned herself to resist applauding. Carl coughed and a strand of spaghetti escaped his lips. Mama's mouth dropped open and she brought her hand up, pressing it to her bosom. An anguished, martyred expression came to her face.

"I can't believe it," she whined. "I can't believe it. That man of yours, Leona May, told me to shut up! No one has ever told Mama Wadonelli to shut up!" She pounded her breast with a fist.

Herbie shoved his chair backwards and stood up abruptly. "I do the best I know how. No one starves in my family. I bring home my check to Leona May every second Tuesday of the month. I work hard." His voice cracked and he cleared his throat. "Sometimes sixteen hours a day. I'm good to my wife and my kids. Five kids take a lot of care and money so I get the best payin' job I can. And that's truckin'. I fathered five healthy kids." He sighed. "I ... I do the best I can." A pout came to his thin lips.

Mama looked at him and nodded. "That is true. Leona May, that is true. He did father five bambinos. More stars in both of your crowns for that. And you don't prevent the blessed event of pregnancy like so many of those misguided Catholics these days." She swung her head to Herbie. "You ever think about joining our Church or any church for that matter?"

Herbie looked at Leona May to make a reply for him. Leona May looked at Mama and then at Herbie and then again at Mama.

"I'm not asking your wife. I'm asking you," Mama reminded him.

"I ... I am thinkin' about it. Maybe ... maybe."

Mama threw her hands up to the heavens. "Praise God! Praise God!" She pulled her hanky from her sleeve and sobbed into it. "Leona May's husband is going to be one of us."

Herbie shifted uneasily from one foot to the other. "Mama ... I haven't yet. I ... I ... I need time."

"Of course you do. But God is guiding you now; I can tell. He will guide you to do the right thing. Sit ... sit down!" Mama gestured. "Leona May, pass the spaghetti to your husband."

A huge grin broke out on Herbie's homely face. He slid back into his chair and tucked his napkin under his chin.

"Carl ... Joan ... pass the bread and salad down here to Leona May's husband. This boy is hungry. He's a hard working father of five bambinos." Mama scooped huge mounds of each dish onto Herbie's plate. "More salad, Herbert?" Mama blew her nose and looked at Leona May. "God is good, Leona May ... God is good."

Leona May rushed to Herbie's side and placed her arms around his neck.

Mama sighed and looked wistfully to the ceiling.

Leona May continued to nuzzle the back of Herbie's neck as he bent forward to eat. She finally looked up to Mama. "What,

Mama … what? Just a moment ago you were so happy. What is it, Mama?"

Mama heaved a deep breath and wiped between her first and second chins. "Praise, Jesus. He must think Mama is never happy … never satisfied. Papa is shaking his head in shame from above."

"What, Mama? What is wrong?"

Mama shook her head emphatically. "No … no, I can't say it. Jesus has been too good to Mama, already. No more tonight."

Leona May came to Mama's side and pecked her cheek. "Tell what you are thinkin' about, Mama. We all want to hear it."

Mama shook her head again. "No … no!" She crossed herself and looked to the heavens. "This prayer I've been repeating every night for five months. Jesus is tired of hearing it. Mama wears Him down."

"Tell us what your prayers have been these last five months," Leona May begged in a nasal whine.

Mama smiled sheepishly. "You know Mama's pride in being a Catholic. She wants all of her children to follow God's church as well. Of course, I pray for this as did Papa when he was alive." She crossed herself. "But a prayer even stronger, even said more often, even more impassioned was … God forgive me."

A tear seeped from Mama's right eye and rolled down the valleys of her face. "I pray that God will perform another miracle for Carl and Joan. I have been praying to our God in Heaven to grant them another fine son like the precious one they lost." She turned and looked at Carl and Joan, her eyes brimming with tears.

Chapter 5

Carl and Joan traveled for miles without saying anything to one another. Each of them were submerged in their separate thoughts. The old GMC truck rattled and creaked whenever it hit a pothole or bump in the highway. Carl never explained the cause of the cracked windshield to Joan. He laid awake many nights thinking about that strange event. He knew that extreme loneliness and the agony of missing Ricky could cause him to hallucinate. That was the only sane, rational explanation, wasn't it? There are no visions these days and besides when they do happen, they happen on a mystical mountain top or grassy meadow in places like Spain or Italy. They don't happen on a rocky back road in Kansas.

But, it had seemed so real ... so very real. There Ricky was with that big grin and his front teeth missing and those sparkling, inquisitive eyes. He was running and laughing. And then he disappeared in the twin beams of the truck lights.

That night, two months ago, Carl laid in the pasture for over an hour venting his agonizing sadness and anger. His clothes were dirty and torn and his hands were raw from beating the hard soil in sorrow. He finally sat up when he saw the headlights start to flicker and dim. Surprisingly, the motor turned over allowing him to back down the incline and then weave and buffet his way back onto the road. He got out and mended the downed fence before continuing home. Even a vision was not going to allow him to forget his duty as a responsible farmer.

Traveling home, he felt drained and noticed that the tight, constricted ball of sorrow lodged in his gut for the last three months had strangely been exorcised. He continued home at a safe rate of fifty miles per hour.

Joan's thoughts floated back over their strange day with Mama, Leona May, Herbie and the kids. She always felt as if she had been mauled by a tiger after visiting Mama in Kansas City. Emotions soared and plummeted from one moment to the next in that house. She was relieved it was over.

But, the one thing Joan was sure of was that Mama was sincere when it came to her love and pride of Ricky. She recalled the many times she had pulled him into her ponderous bosom practically suffocating him. She had loved him with every fiber of her volatile, Italian being. She loved and admired him because he was a perfect creation of God. Mama knew that these people were very special in God's eyes.

Then Joan's thoughts went to Leona May's husband, Herbie. She smiled to herself realizing that she also addressed him in the same way Mama does. He finally, today, after twelve years of horrendous treatment, had stood up for himself. A bit meekly granted, but it was the first time. He had scored a victory of sorts today. A smile came to Joan's lips in the darkness. Good for Leona May's husband, Herbie, she thought.

Joan recalled the comforting, maternal feeling of holding Little Joey. He had the same coppery, sweaty smell that she remembered Ricky always had when he was racing about. She had reveled in the bone and flesh of him. It had felt good looking into his little boy's eyes filled with wonder and trust.

Yes, Leona May's kids could drive a tee-tottler to drink, but they were that way because of the lax and inconsistent discipline and because of the sheer, overwhelming task of trying to raise five children between the ages of eleven months and eleven years almost by herself. Leona May had five children in twelve years and Joan thought in all probability she would have ten or twelve snot-nosed little half-Italians running wild throughout the house and throughout her life. The lucky woman, she thought. And there she was, only given one. A perfect one, granted … but only one. And now he was gone. Leona May, with her vast brood of untamed hellions and she with none and no prospects of ever having another.

Suddenly, Joan choked and pressed the palm of her hand against her mouth.

Carl swung his head around. "You okay, honey?"

Joan removed her hand and took a deep breath. "I'm okay. I … I just thought I was getting car sick or something. I guess I'm tired."

"We should be home in another hour. I want you to sleep in tomorrow. I noticed how exhausted you looked when we left Mama's. I'll take care of the chickens tomorrow."

"I'm fine, Carl … really."

"Are you over your headache?"

"How did you know I had a headache?" Joan asked.

"Don't you always have a headache when we go to Mama's? Besides, I saw you rubbing your forehead."

Joan reached over and pressed his hand. "You know me very well, Mr. Wadonelli."

Carl turned and kissed her cheek. "My pleasure, Mrs. Wadonelli."

Joan lay back and closed her eyes. At times she sensed the beams of light of oncoming traffic through her lidded eyes. "That little Joey is some kid. He never rests."

"None of them do. Did you ever see such a pack of hellers in your life?"

Joan giggled. "No, not exactly." She sat forward. "But, you know, Carl, they aren't really that bad. They just don't have any structure or stability with Leona May so excitable and Herbie gone all of the time on the road. It really isn't their fault."

"Yeah, I was thinking … Maybe we could have two of the oldest boys come out to the farm later on and spend some time. Would you like that?"

Joan fell silent.

"Did I say something wrong?" Carl asked.

"No, of course not. I just don't know. What if we get attached. How would we let them go?"

"I just meant for a few days … a week at the most."

"Oh, of course. I guess that would be fine. They need to get out of the city to some place where they can run. It would do them a world of good and give Leona May a break as well."

"We'll talk about it."

Joan leaned forward and faced Carl. She nervously cleared her throat. "Could we talk about something else?"

"Sure," Carl said, casually. "What is it?"

"Well," Joan said, hesitantly, digging at a thumbnail, "I did something three weeks ago that I should have talked over with you first."

"What is that? If you bought some new clothes and charged it, that's fine. We'll manage. And besides, if it makes you feel …"

"It's not new clothes, Carl. Besides, my clothes are fine."

"Well, then, what?" His eyes concentrated on the oncoming traffic."

"Well, you know I've been seeing Father Shawn for quite awhile now. I didn't want to go back after that first time, but I'm glad I did."

Carl reached over searching for her hand in the dark. "I know. I think it's helping you, don't you?"

"I do think it is. He's been very patient and kind. He made me realize that God didn't take Ricky from us. Ricky took himself from us by his act of trying to swim in that rain-swollen pond that day in April. God is as sad as we are. For a long time, I wouldn't listen to any of that. But, lately, I really think that's the way it is. We have a free will. God gives us a free will."

"I'm glad you see it that way, hon. I can tell you, I didn't say a whole lot, but I had a lot of anger too."

"Father Shawn made me realize that anger was okay for the first few months, but if it didn't lessen, in time it would make me remote and bitter and no one would benefit from it. It could finally eat a person alive."

"I'm glad he helped you, Joan. I've been worried about you for so long. Father Shawn's a good man and a darned good boxer." He laid his head back and laughed.

"But, Carl, that isn't really what I wanted to talk to you about on the way home tonight."

"Oh, something else?"

"Yes."

"Go ahead. Hit me with it."

"Well, that first time I went to see him two months ago, Father Shawn asked me if we had ever thought of having another child. I told him that we had a terrible time having Ricky. And it would almost take a miracle for me to get pregnant again, especially now that we're both years older. I told him we had reconciled ourselves to remaining childless. Then he asked me if we had ever thought of taking in a foster child or even adopting."

"Foster child ... adoption ...?"

"Now, hear me out before you say no." She scooted close to him and placed her arm around his shoulder. "We have a lot to offer a baby, don't we? I mean, we are good, moral people. We're not rich, but we're not dirt poor either. We've got plenty of room in our house. And a farm is a great place to raise a child." She played with the lobe of his ear. "And Carl, I know there's children out there needing a place to live ... needing a family. Father Shawn said the need was great, in fact. We could offer a balance of stability and love."

"You sound as though you've thought quite a lot about all of this."

"At first, I dismissed it right away. I felt it would be disloyal to Ricky somehow. I didn't want anyone ever taking his place in our lives. But as time went on and I made more and more visits to Father Shawn and read the scriptures that he assigned and prayed about it, I slowly changed. I agreed with him that we did have a lot to offer a child. And it wasn't disloyal to Ricky at all. Ricky will always be with us in our hearts. And why shouldn't we help out a little kid who is abandoned or abused or whatever?"

"Are there babies needing homes?"

Joan opened her purse and placed it near the panel lights. She fished around in the bottom of it. "Ah, here it is," she said. She held up the wrinkled, limp business card. "Catholic Charities in Stockton. A Sister Angelica is the director."

"So, do you want to look into this, Joan?"

"I've already done that. That's what I meant when I said I did something three weeks ago that I should have talked to you about first. I called and they sent me some forms to fill out. I filled them out and sent them back two weeks ago."

"All this without saying one word to me?"

"I'm sorry, hon. I know I should have talked with you. But, I was afraid that you would talk me out of it. Please don't be mad."

"I'm not mad, Joan. Besides, it's just an inquiry at this point. We're not obligated."

"Yes, that's right. Anyway, I got a call two days ago while you were milking, and … and …"

Carl turned to her. "… and what?"

"We have an appointment with Sister Angelica at St. Vincents tomorrow at two o'clock!"

Carl shifted about in the large, black leather chair. It squeaked with every movement he made. He looked around at the large high-ceilinged office and then at the solid, heavy furniture. He approved of the aura of stability and no-nonsense. He never felt comfortable in an office with frills and flimsy furniture. That was for college girls' apartments, he thought, not for places where important decisions had to be made. Places like banks, farm extensions and cooperatives had that no-nonsense look. His eyes wandered to the worn, somber gray carpet showing its years and miles of foot traffic. And then he looked up again at the large wooden crucifix behind a cluttered desk. Nothing extravagant, he thought. It was as it should be.

Carl and Joan jumped as the door opened and a nun entered with a smile and a nod of her head.

"Sister Angelica will be here directly," she said. "She told me to tell you to make yourselves comfortable."

Joan and Carl smiled as the black, flowing habit backed out of the door.

"Sisters of Charity, isn't it?" Joan asked, distractedly searching through her handbag for a compact. She flicked it open and peered into the mirror smoothing her hair with an upsweep of her hand. "My hair look okay?" She didn't wait for an answer. "Virgie got it too tight this time." She stood up with her back to Carl and looked over her shoulder. "Seams straight? I didn't know whether to wear my gray wool or my black crepe with the lace collar. I wore these little pearl earrings. I'm trying to appear as conservative as possible."

Carl smiled and reached for her hand. "Calm down, Joan. You look fine." He drew deep on his cigarette and expelled the smoke through expanded nostrils.

Joan peered down with a frown. "Don't tell me that. First impressions make a lot of difference to these people. Why do you think I wore my gold cross pendant?" She snatched the cigarette from his lips and crushed it out in a tray on the desk. "Don't smoke while you're in here."

"Okay, sorry." Carl sat up straight and adjusted his tie. He felt as if it were choking him.

Joan walked over and sat down beside him. "I'm sorry, too. I just want to please her. I've been a Catholic all my life and I still get a little skittish when I see them in their long, black habits. Most of them at my school were real sweet." She shook her head. "I guess they still intimidate me a little, that's all."

"Joan, you told me you put everything down truthful on those forms. You did, didn't you?"

"Yes, of course."

"Okay. You told them about our religious preference, our finances, and our morals. We don't have any criminal records or contagious diseases. We're honest, upright citizens."

"Sure, we're all of that and we're also forty years old."

"We're still good people who can give a kid a good home and that's what they're interested in."

The door swung open and Sister Angelica entered in a rush. Her face was flushed and beaded with sweat. She swept her habit close to her and sat down in a swivel chair behind the desk. She placed several papers in front of her and then looked up over a pair of bifocals. She extended her hand. "Mr. Wadonelli … Mrs. Wadonelli … A warm, genuine smile coated her ruddy, full-moon face. She stood and reached across the desk to receive their hands.

"Please sit down, Mr. and Mrs. Wadonelli."

Carl sank back into his chair but Joan remained nervously perched on the edge.

Sister Angelica picked the forms up and poked her glasses back onto the bridge of her nose. She cleared her throat. "First of all, let me convey my deepest sympathy on the loss of your only child five months ago."

Carl and Joan nodded and mumbled their thank yous.

"I have gone over your forms very carefully, Mr. and Mrs. Wadonelli. I should correct myself. My committee and I have gone over your forms. We think that God is smiling on you today. How generous and kind of you to want to care for someone else's child."

"We do need a child in our lives, Sister," Carl offered.

Sister Angelica nodded with a look of sympathy. "Here at St. Vincents we try to be very careful to place our children in good Catholic homes. Even though being a Catholic is not a stringent prerequisite, it is surely an advantage when it comes to choosing our prospective parents." She ran a large index finger along item number twelve on the first form. "I see, Mr. Wadonelli, that you are self-employed."

"That's right, Sister. I have a section and a half of land in Cawker County. It's the family farm. My dad farmed it before I took over. We're still paying one of the quarters off, but we make the payments just as regular as clockwork in spite of the drought and the low prices."

"That's very commendable, Mr. Wadonelli."

"Yes, Sister, we both work very hard. I help in the field, milk, and take care of my chickens as well as take care of the house, but once we have a baby I can assure you, my main focus would be with that baby. Carl would just have to do without my help for a few years. I think raising a baby takes priority," Joan said with conviction.

Sister Angelica looked up and wrinkled her nose and then pushed at her glasses. "I certainly don't mean to embarrass you, Mrs. Wadonelli, but I see it says here it's impossible for you to have any more children."

Joan lowered her eyes. "It doesn't embarrass us at all. I had a terrible time conceiving. It took years of tests and treatments. And then once I did I had a terrible time carrying him. I had had many miscarriages before. So, I spent the last four months in bed before delivery." She smiled. "Of course, it was worth it."

"The doctors have told us that it would be next to impossible to have another child. And then again there's our ages to consider," Carl said, shifting uncomfortably in his leather chair.

Sister Angelica smiled warmly. "Please do not think it is just my idle curiosity. It's just one of the many questions we ask of all prospective parents when they are older than our usual parents-to-be. My committee will ask, I am sure, when I meet with them again."

"You see, Sister, at first we reconciled ourselves to live our lives childless after losing Ricky. And then as time went by and I kept visiting with Father Shawn and my anger and sorrow eased a bit we knew that our lives will never be complete or fulfilled without a child. We could give a baby a very good home," Joan said leaning forward.

Sister Angelica sobered, but nodded with understanding. "Yes, I know what you are saying. I thank God every day that I was granted the right to work with children. I will never have any of my own and being involved with children and parents helps fulfill my needs, I suppose." She looked longingly to the ceiling lost for a moment in the thoughts of the past. A flush came to her face and she repositioned the fan to get some air. "Oh, what am I doing? I didn't mean to interject my own circumstances into the meeting. Please, forgive me. I suppose my point is that I do understand, Mrs. and Mrs. Wadonelli, how life can be so barren … so unfulfilling without a child. I marvel at your strength and courage to come to us now especially after the tragedy of losing your own child. Surely God has guided you."

"I think God, Father Shawn, and maybe Leona May's kids." Joan looked at Carl and winked.

Carl chuckled.

Joan became serious. "So, if we can't have another child of our own naturally, we would very happily accept a baby of some-one else's to raise and love as our own."

"Most admirable of you, Mrs. Wadonelli. I'm sure you and Mr. Wadonelli could provide a wonderful home for a child."

"Well, it isn't as if I've never taken care of a baby before. I raised Ricky until … Well, anyway, I took care of my brothers years ago, also. I was the oldest in the family. So I knew all about bottles, diapers, midnight feedings, and rashes. And Carl is a great father. He would play with the child, take him fishing, play ball with him … work with him. Everyone would be so happy for us, especially Mama Wadonelli who has prayed for us for the last five months." She took a breath and continued. "And we're very faithful Catholics. We never miss mass and holy days of obliga-tion. I could even teach religious education later on …" Joan looked at Sister Angelica and then at Carl feeling a rush of embarrassment coat her face. She knew she was trying too hard.

Sister Angelica nodded in agreement. "I'm sure both of you would be excellent parents." She paused and clasped her hands together on the desk.

Carl and Joan sat forward in their chairs preparing them-selves.

"I know you both realize how many people are waiting for new-born babies. We have a waiting list that will take at least three to four years to fill."

A sick feeling came to the pit of Joan's stomach. "Our ages are against us, aren't they, Sister?"

Sister Angelica looked sympathetic. "Of course, I must be honest in such an important matter. Your ages were certainly discussed when the committee met last week. We are sure your intentions are genuine and we would love, with the help of God, to place a newborn baby in your home."

"But, it's impossible, right?" Joan asked quietly.

Carl nodded sadly. "It's kind of what I expected, Sister, even though I didn't tell Joan. I thought there was always that hope."

Sister Angelica's eyes clouded with tears for a moment. She coughed shyly and tried to compose herself. "It always hurts me so much when I must tell people these things."

Joan sighed and got to her feet. "Well, we appreciate you being open and honest."

"I'm so sorry, Mr. and Mrs. Wadonelli. I would love to help you. I think you would make very fine parents."

Joan shrugged. "That's okay; we understand. Nothing ventured, nothing gained as the old saying goes. I guess Pete will have to be our complete family."

Carl walked toward Sister Angelica and extended his hand. "It was great meeting you, Sister. Thank you for your time."

Joan shook hands with Sister Angelica and turned toward the door. Carl encircled her shoulders.

Sister Angelica picked up the forms, shuffled them and prepared to file them. Suddenly, she stiffened and turned with an intense look. "Wait! Wait, Mr. and Mrs. Wadonelli!"

Carl and Joan stopped in mid-stride.

"I promised myself that I wouldn't mention it, but I just had to. It is as though God is directing me to."

Carl and Joan looked at her, puzzled.

"What if we could place a child older than a baby? You could get this child immediately."

Carl's face broke into a grin. Joan eased herself into a hard-back chair feeling her legs weaken.

"Would you be willing to accept an older child ... a boy?"

Joan looked at Carl. She grasped his hand and squeezed. Tears pushed out of the corners of her eyes. In her mind she saw a replication of Ricky: bright smile, inquisitive sparkling eyes ... white hair blowing in the wind ...

"Sister, we would of course, accept a boy older than a baby. Two or three years old would be great. He'd be that much closer to playing baseball," Carl said, his hopes soaring.

All of them laughed together.

"Oh, yes, Sister, a little boy would be wonderful. When can we see him?" Joan asked, excitedly.

"You can see him today if you would like, but I want to explain some things about him." She cleared her throat nervously. "First of all, he's older than two or three."

"How old is he, Sister?" Carl asked with beginning doubt.

Sister Angelica looked reluctantly over her glasses. She patted the perspiration on her forehead with her handkerchief. "Hot in here, isn't it? Well, he's … twelve years old."

"Oh!" Joan put her fist to her mouth.

Carl shook his head. "Oh, I don't know. That's pretty old. They're pretty grown up already and they're set in their ways. I was driving a tractor at that age. Is he a juvenile delinquent or what? Why have his folks given him up?"

Sister Angelica fondled the cross around her neck nervously. "He has no father. At least, no one knows who he is. His mother was killed out on route 67 in a one car accident three weeks ago. Thank God, he was not with her."

"What about relatives?" Carl asked. "Why doesn't he go to them?"

"They don't want him. It seems nobody wants him. We've contacted everybody. That's why he's here."

Joan winced. "How sad. The poor little tyke."

"Yes, he's all alone. He needs a family so badly. He needs parents so badly. He was brought here by the authorities when none of the relatives would accept him. In fact, we haven't even found a foster home that would accept him. He's very frightened."

"But, he's just too old, Sister. We wanted a little one … even two or three years old. But one that's twelve. I just don't know." Joan pressed her fingers to her temple in thought.

"It would just be on a trial basis, of course. Perhaps a month or so. Like a foster home. He just needs a chance," Sister Angelica posed.

Carl frowned. "Wait a minute. It sounds to me like there is more to this than you're revealing."

"Carl, you shouldn't talk to Sister Angelica like that," Joan admonished.

Sister Angelica waved her hand. "No … no, Mr. Wadonelli is right. There is something that I'm not telling you. I'm finding it very difficult to explain."

"Is the kid a delinquent. Is he a thief or something?" Carl asked.

"Barry, that's the boy's name," Sister Angelica looked up at the crucifix on the wall and crossed herself reverently. "… is mentally handicapped. He is a mongoloid better known these days as Down Syndrome. He requires special help and schooling."

Joan grabbed her handbag and started toward the door. "Oh, no you don't! Forget it!"

Carl nodded. "I agree with Joan, Sister. We aren't saddling ourselves with a kid that's retarded. We've got enough trouble without that."

"But, he's one of God's children too. Please, at least meet him. He's a real charmer. At least let him come in to meet you. He has a right to have parents too!" Sister Angelica's forehead creased in frustration as sweat trailed down her face.

Carl and Joan opened the door and started to leave. Sister Angelica gathered up the bottom of her habit and rushed forward catching Carl's shoulder. She held him tight. "I'm not letting you leave until you meet him. I've been planning this meeting ever since I first read your application. You and Mrs. Wadonelli would be perfect for Barry."

Carl tried to pull loose, but she grappled him back into the vice-like hold. She placed a foot up on the door holding it shut. Joan stood there, staring, with her hands on her hips.

"Please, Mr. and Mrs. Wadonelli, give him a chance. God and I both plead with you," she gasped still holding tight to Carl's shoulder.

"Carl, for crying out loud! You're wrestling with a nun!" Joan screamed in disbelief.

"Okay, Sister, okay! Bring him in here!" Carl shouted.

Sister Angelica released him. "Oh, praise God for keeping you here."

Carl rotated his sore shoulder. "It wasn't God, Sister. It was your hammerlock."

Sister Angelica winced in shame. "I'm sorry, Mr. Wadonelli. It's just that I've been praying for this moment ever since Barry came here three weeks ago on the same day we received your application papers. It was as though it was meant to be. God's will has to be helped now and then." She walked over to the intercom and contacted the outer office. She stood erect, behind her desk fondling her gold cross, waiting for the door to open.

Carl straightened his clothes. He and Joan stared at the closed door. At last, the door opened and the same young nun who came in before entered holding a boy's hand. Barry stood there, blinking his slanted eyes. There was not a hair on his head. He scrunched up his face as though there was something distasteful about the whole situation. He was much shorter and stockier than the average twelve-year-old boy. He looked at Carl and Joan closely. Finally, he opened his mouth and stuck out his cracked tongue. "Is this my new dad and mom?" he asked in a gutteral voice.

Sister Angelica glowed with satisfaction standing behind her desk with her arms folded.

Chapter 6

Joan lowered her newspaper and peered across the room at Carl. He stared straight ahead into space. There was a shocked expression on his face. She watched him carefully over her paper as he lit a cigarette and blew smoke from his flared nostrils. A surge of sorrow ran through her as she looked at his sad face. Finally, she laid the paper aside and bent over to scratch Pete behind the ears. Pete moaned with contentment.

"Did you hear Pete growl when we brought him in tonight?" Joan shook her head. "I don't think Pete has ever growled at anyone before in his entire life."

Carl drew on his cigarette in thought.

"It isn't exactly the way we planned, is it? He isn't the cute, little cherub dressed in blue booties. Of course, he is bald like a new baby. That's one thing, I guess." Joan attempted a chuckle but gagged. "Oh, Carl, what've we done?"

Carl shook his head. "That nun was something else. She had one of the best hammerlocks I've ever seen."

"What about tomorrow? I have to go into town. I don't know if I dare take him. I wonder if his mother took him out. He looks so strange. Did you see him tonight? He kind of grinds his food and slobbers in it. And that crack right down the middle of his tongue turns my stomach." Joan slapped her mouth. "Would you listen to me? I'm talking about this poor kid who's just lost his mother. Doesn't he have enough against him without me giving him a hard time?"

Carl nodded. "I know what you mean, Joan. There isn't a mean bone in your body when it comes to kids. I saw the way you handled Donna Marie and Little Joey the other night at Mama's. You're a natural mother."

Joan smiled to herself.

"What? What're you thinking about?"

"Here I was trying to make such a good impression on Sister Angelica. I wore my most conservative clothes. Even had my hair done. I did everything I was supposed to do." She pointed at Carl. "And you ... I took the cigarette away from you and put it out. It serves me right for putting on such airs. God must've pointed right at me and said 'get her and that husband of hers' for lying to a nun.' I deserve everything I got ... except this."

"Wait a minute, hon. This isn't a life sentence. The kid's only visiting for a month. That was the deal. It's just getting him out of there for a little while, that's all. That's all we promised."

"Wouldn't you know, Carl, that we'd get the booby prize. Two old duds like us wanting to be parents again. You might know we'd end up with the lost link ... a twelve-year-old mongoloid, whatever that is."

Carl rolled his eyes back in thought. "As I understand it from what Sister Angelica said, it's a kind of retardation. All of them that have it have the same things wrong with them. She said that every cell in their body is damaged. Isn't that strange?"

"Well, I don't care one way or the other. Why didn't I hold my ground and tell her that it was no deal, no matter what? Of course, it's a shame. Nobody deserves what he's got in life and then to top it off, his mother is killed." Joan shook her head. "No one should have to put up with all of that. I'm just too soft-hearted for my own good. All I had to do was to walk out of that office and refuse." She brushed her hands together. "Just refuse, that's all. I don't care if she can wrestle like Gorgeous George. If we don't want to do it, we don't do it."

"Well, Joan, we're in it for a month. Come thirty days from today, we'll pack him up bag and baggage and trot him right back to St. Vincents and to Sister Angelica."

Joan sighed. "At least he's asleep. He does know how to undress himself and put his pajamas on." She shuddered. "I get almost ill when I think he's sleeping in Ricky's bed."

Carl smiled. "You know, I went in to help him get his pajamas on and he doesn't have a hair on him … not one. Bald from head to toe. What a strange looking kid."

"Yes, that's against him, too … the way he looks. He even walks kind of hunched over."

The door to Ricky's room opened slowly. Carl and Joan watched as a pair of slanted eyes peeked out from behind it.

"What is it, kid?" Carl asked. "Can't you get to sleep? You're a big boy. Just go back and climb into bed and try it again."

"Maybe he's scared, Carl. You know, strange people and a strange house and all. Call him by name."

Carl walked over to the partially opened door. "Barry, come on out here, kid. There's no reason to be scared." He beckoned with his finger. "Come on out here."

The pair of eyes continued to peer out from the dark room.

Joan got up and walked over to the door, reached in, and grabbed Barry's hand. She was jolted hard from the other side and her head thudded against the door. She caught his hand again and struggled to pull him from the room. Carl watched the tug-of-war, fascinated, for a time. Finally, Barry was pulled into the living room, his eyes blinking to adjust them to the sudden light. A dark wet spot was at his crotch. Carl and Joan looked at each other and then at Barry.

Barry blinked his eyes on the verge of tears and lowered his head with shame. "I … I pissed my pants."

Joan tried to look stern. "Young man, you aren't supposed to use words like that. It isn't nice."

Barry looked up, mortified. "I not mean to. I not know where the bathroom was." His lower lip quivered and he gave way to deep sobs.

Carl walked over to him and bent over to look him in the eyes. "Now, kid, quit crying. It isn't the end of the world. I should have showed you where the bathroom was."

"Carl, why don't you take him in and get him a fresh pair of pajamas," Joan suggested.

Carl took Barry by the hand and led him back into Ricky's room. "Do you have to use the bathroom now?" he asked.

Barry scrunched up his face and stuck out his tongue. "Not now, Mr. Wadi."

"My name is Mr. Wadonelli." He leaned down. "Say it slow for me, kid. Wad-o-nell-i."

Barry concentrated hard. "Wad-o ... Wad-o ... "

Carl leaned closer and peered into Barry's round face. "Wad-o-nell-i, Wad-o-nell-i; it's Italian. Try it once more. Wad-o-nell-i. Wad ..." He pointed to Barry.

"Wad." Barry said in a gravel voice.

"O."

"O."

"Nell."

"Nell."

"I."

"I."

"Now, what is it, kid? Mr. who?"

Barry thought for a moment. "Mr. Who."

Carl hit the side of his head. "Mr. Wadi will be fine."

Barry grinned, pleased with himself.

"Now, climb out of those wet PJ's and get into some dry ones."

Barry started to obey.

Carl pulled Barry's suitcase out from under the bed, opened it, and dug for a pair of dry pajamas. Buried at the bottom of the suitcase was an old toy dog, one ear was missing and tufts of stuffing protruded from torn seams.

Barry grabbed the dog from him and rubbed it lovingly along his face. "My dog, Toto. My dog, Toto."

Carl winced. "Hey, you're too old to play with stuffed animals. That's baby stuff!" He reached for the dog, but Barry lurched backward and held on to the dog protectively.

"No! You leave Toto alone!" He held the toy to him.

"Here, let me have that thing. You're going to act like a man when you're in my house, kid." Carl reached for it again and grabbed its good ear. A ripping sound was heard and he found the torn ear in his hand.

Barry's eyes narrowed with hate. He stuck out his cracked tongue and started to scream. "Mr. Wadi ... damn you! Damn Wadi."

Carl tried to place the torn ear back on the dog's head. "I'm sorry. I'm real sorry. I didn't mean to tear your toy. But only babies have toys like that. You've got to understand."

Barry shook his head emphatically and stomped his feet. "Mr. Wadi ... damn you! Damn ... Mr. Wadi!"

"Now don't get hysterical. We can fix it. Here, let me see it."

Barry ran to a corner of the room clutching the dog, crying.

Joan opened the door with an abrupt jerk. "What in the world is going on in here? It sounds like you're killing the kid."

Carl made a futile effort to explain above Barry's wails.

Joan went over to Barry. "What is it? What did Mr. Wadonelli do to you?"

Barry held out his stuffed animal and pointed to the absent ear.

Joan turned with a scornful look on her face. "Oh, for crying out loud. Why did you tear the kid's toy?"

Carl had a sheepish look on his face. "I didn't mean to. I just reached for it and it accidentally came off."

Barry rubbed the stuffed dog against his face and moaned with contentment.

Joan watched him for a moment. "It looks like that old toy has been with him for a long time. It probably reminds him of his home or his mother." She held out her hand for the stuffed dog and Barry reluctantly gave it to her. Joan walked over to Ricky's dresser, pulled out a drawer, and searched for a safety pin. Carl handed her the torn ear and she fastened it to the dog once again. She handed it back to Barry. A grin lit up his face as he hugged the toy.

"Thank you, thank you, Mrs. Wadi."

Joan nodded and patted his shoulder. "Now, you get into those dry pajamas and I'll put on some fresh bedding."

Barry lay the little dog on the pillow and started to push his pajama bottoms down. Joan turned her back preparing the bed.

"It doesn't bother him one bit," Carl said. "He doesn't care that a strange woman is going to see him naked. What a strange kid."

Joan continued making the bed. "He's just a kid, Carl. He probably thinks of me as a woman like his mother. Every mother sees their children naked."

"Still, a boy that age generally dies of shame if a strange woman sees him naked. I know Ricky would have."

Barry paid no attention to the conversation as he bit his tongue while he concentrated on buttoning his pajama tops.

"Is he through yet, Carl?" Joan peered over her shoulder and then turned around. "Now, you get yourself into bed and get some sleep."

Barry crawled into bed and scooted under the covers. He placed Toto on the pillow next to him.

Joan looked down and tucked the blankets snugly around him. "Now, it's getting late. The bathroom is right across the hall there, so if you have to use it, go ahead. I'll leave the lamp on in the living room."

Barry scrunched up his face and stuck out his tongue. Joan began to realize that sticking out his tongue was a gesture meaning that he was pleased or unsure. She switched off the light as they turned to leave.

"Mrs. Wadi." Barry held out his arms. "Mrs. Wadi ... kiss."

Joan turned back and looked down at the dark silhouette. "What? You want me to give you a good night kiss? Did your mother used to kiss you good night?"

"Mama kiss me night time ... now, Mrs. Wadi kiss Barry night time."

Joan bent down and kissed Barry on the cheek.

"Night, Mrs. Wadi ... night, Mr. Wadi." Barry snuggled the ragged dog to his face and closed his eyes.

Joan nodded for Carl to follow her carefully out of the room. Carl closed the door easily behind him. He started to speak but noticed a finger at Joan's lips. She motioned toward Ricky's bedroom.

###

Barry sat on a stool close to the kitchen at the Blue Bird Cafe. Carl needed to pick up some supplies in town late in the day and Barry happily agreed to come along. Carl told Joan that he and Barry would grab the special at the Blue Bird today, so she wouldn't have to worry about getting supper. Carl was a regular at the cafe and knew the owner and workers well.

Barry watched Benny, a skinny high school kid in a tee-shirt, jeans, and paper cap push a pile of dishes under a mound of steaming suds. Barry was fascinated by the shifting of his bony buttocks as he reached for more dirty dishes, submerged them, scrubbed them and then scalded them. Benny, looked around once in a while and stared with curiosity at Barry. Barry stuck his tongue out and smiled. Each time Benny turned back abruptly as though he had been caught in a misdeed.

Barry seemed to enjoy the smells escaping from the kitchen. They ranged from the sharp, pungent smell of vinegar, to the tantalizing smell of deep fried onion rings, to the rank smell of human sweat.

Once in a while, the delicious aroma of hot biscuits wafted from the kitchen and made his mouth water. He sat on the stool quietly and obediently waiting for his order of salisbury steak to arrive because Mr. Wadi had told him to.

Barry's hazy mind had difficulty keeping up with the newness of sounds, smells, and people. He grimaced and tried to understand, but never quite did. All he knew was that he liked being in the cafe and the hot biscuits smelled delicious.

Benny walked into the serving area wiping his forehead with the bottom of his wet and stained apron. He filled a glass with ice and poured a Coca Cola into it. He stood there sipping it, staring at Barry who was staring intently back at him.

"Something the matter?" Carl asked.

Benny's face flushed. "No, not at all, Mr. Wadonelli. I'm just taking a little break. Been on my feet for over three hours straight."

"You were staring at the kid, here," Carl said accusingly.

Benny winced and rolled his eyes toward Barry. "I don't want him to hear me," he whispered. "I ain't never been around these kind before. He makes me nervous. He just stares at me and grins."

Carl looked down at Barry. Barry scrunched up his face, stuck out his tongue, and smiled.

Benny pointed. "See what I mean? That's all he's been doin' for the past half hour. I can't work when someone like that is lookin' at me."

A muscle in Carl's jaw flexed. "Someone like what?" He was a bit confused as to why he was feeling defensive.

Benny fidgeted with his apron bib. "You know; someone dull-witted like that."

Blood surged to Carl's face. "He isn't dull-witted, as you call it. The kid is mentally handicapped."

"No disrespect, Mr. Wadonelli, but I don't see the difference."

"The difference is in the way you say it. He's just like us except he has trouble … thinking."

Benny looked quickly at Barry and then away. "Yeah, but he looks funny. He kinda looks Chinese or something."

Carl pulled on the bill of his cap with annoyance. "Every cell is damaged in his body. But, he can still do things … a lot of things."

"He can?" Benny asked curiously. "Like what?"

"He can dress himself and go to the bathroom by himself and …" Carl thought for a moment. "… and he can tie his shoes if you give him time."

"That ain't much for a kid his age."

Carl grabbed Benny roughly by the arm and pulled him over to Barry.

Barry looked up, blinking. Carl plucked Benny's paper hat off his head, adjusted it, and set it on Barry's bald head. "Kid," he said, "this guy is Benny. He thinks he's a dishwasher. Shake hands with him."

Benny placed his hands behind his back. Barry reached out to shake hands, but Benny refused. Barry grimaced and stuck out his tongue.

"Tell you what, kid, you get over there and show this guy how a real dish washer works."

Barry looked up with a confused expression. Carl pointed to the huge stack of dishes. Barry broke out into an ear-to-ear grin. He walked to the sink in a hunched gait. Carl crossed his arms and watched. Barry crawled up on a wooden box to reach the top of the stack. He looked around. Then he turned and lunged for the stack of dishes. A waitress screamed and grabbed her mouth as the stack of dishes teetered back and forth. Carl watched, frozen with dread, as the dishes leaned to one side and then to the other and finally crashed to the floor. Barry jumped off the box and jumped up and down, clapping his hands with delight.

Carl rushed up to Barry, grabbed him by the shoulder and guided him away from the broken glass. He pushed down on his head, flattening his paper cap. Barry looked up at Carl's menacing stare, grimaced and stuck out his tongue.

Customers lined the serving window to the kitchen to view the commotion.

Carl turned and shrugged. "It was the dishwasher's fault for stacking them that high in the first place," he explained. Turning, he looked at the people watching the retarded boy and the pile of broken dishes on the floor.

"What's this look like ... a sideshow? Go on back to your seats!" Carl yelled.

Carl threw down a twenty dollar bill. "I think that will cover the loss." He and Barry returned to their stools to eat.

Benny shook his head with bewilderment as he went to the closet to get a broom to sweep up the broken glass.

Carl turned, hearing a familiar voice. "Hiya, Wadonelli. How's things goin'?"

Carl looked up seeing Dusty Morton wave at him from two stools down.

"What's all the ruckus back there?" Dusty asked. "It sounded like the beginning of World War II."

Carl shrugged. "Ah, a few dishes fell, that's all."

"I just dropped in to have a burger and to tell you that I'm thinking of having the game at my house in a few weeks. See if you can make it."

"I'll try, Dusty. I'll try," Carl said.

"And no hard feelings for us being such jakes at Charley's awhile back?" Dusty stretched to shake hands.

"No, not at all," Carl said, reaching for Dusty's outstretched hand.

Dusty looked at Barry. "Hey, who's the kid sitting there making faces next to you?"

Benny turned around from his sweeping and looked at Barry. Barry scrunched his face up and stuck out his tongue.

"What a weird lookin' kid," Dusty said, looking closer at Barry. "Is there somethin' wrong with him?"

"Joan and I are looking after him for a few weeks," Carl replied over his shoulder. "His mother was killed out on Highway 67 a few weeks back. He didn't have anywhere to go."

"What a kid to get stuck with." He shook his head. "Oh, well, you and Joan were always suckers for someone in need."

"He's a pretty good kid. He doesn't cause any trouble. It's just a few weeks, then, back he goes."

Dusty picked up his plate and walked over and sat down beside Barry. "What's your name, kid?" he asked.

"Barry," he said in his gravel voice.

"He even sounds funny, doesn't he? He isn't all there, is he, Wadoneli?"

"He's mentally handicapped, Dusty, can't you see that? Use a little tact."

"Okay, I understand. I've read about kids like that. They all look alike, don't they?"

Carl checked his watch and saw that Barry had a lot left to

eat. "Say, Dusty, would you watch the kid for a little while? I've got to run to the creamery before it closes and pick up the egg check. I won't be over fifteen minutes."

"Sure, be glad to. Go ahead, he'll be fine. In fact, I'll buy him a pop." He looked at Barry. "What kind of pop you like, kid?"

Barry looked up at him, scrunched his face, and stuck out his tongue.

Dusty looked at Carl and scowled. "Kid hasn't got any manners, stickin' his tongue out that way when a person is trying to be nice to him."

"He does that when he's ... when he's pleased. It's just one of his habits, that's all," Carl explained.

"What a weird kid." Dusty shook his head. "He's even bald. Has he been sick or somethin'?"

Carl ignored Dusty and leaned down to Barry. "You sit here with this man and finish eating for a few minutes. I've got an errand I've got to take care of. I'll be back real soon and then we'll high-tail it for home."

"He'll be fine, Wadonelli. Don't worry," Dusty said. He looked back down at Barry. "What kind of pop you like? Grape, orange, root beer ...?"

Barry looked puzzled and grimaced.

"What kind ... grape, orange ... root beer?" Dusty repeated.

Barry's eyes opened wide. "Beer ... I like beer!"

Carl shook his head, smiled, and walked out of the cafe door.

Dusty laughed as he motioned for the waitress to bring him a bottle of pop. "Right you are ... beer comin' up ... the root variety."

Carl glanced at his watch. It was getting late. It was time to pick up Barry and get home. As he approached the Blue Bird Cafe he heard the syncopated beat of a rock and roll tune being played on the juke box. He moved his head back and forth to the beat reaching for the door knob. Suddenly, he realized that he felt better than he had in months. At least since Ricky's death. Barry had really been no trouble. He tried his best to feed the chickens, milk, and do his household chores. And in the evening little things pleased him so much. He always complimented Joan on the food she cooked. Small things thrilled him. Watching his clown show on T.V. or sitting beside them as they read him a story pleased him. And of course when he went to bed so did Toto and he always begged for a good night kiss. Perhaps, having the kid around wasn't so bad, at least for a few weeks. Maybe, Carl thought, the kid sort of grew on a person.

Carl swung the door open and stood at the threshold watching the scene taking place in front of the juke box.

Barry swayed back and forth stomping his feet to the music. His face lit up in a grin. He hunched his rounded shoulders swaying and kicking his feet to the music. He faced a row of customers on the stools. Dusty grinned over his shoulder at the men on the stools who were winking and prodding each other with their elbows.

Carl felt sick. He looked at Barry's happy face. He looked at the faces of the customers' grinning mockery. And then he looked at Dusty's toothy grin.

Finally, Carl walked over to the juke box, bent over, and yanked the plug from the wall. The fast beat song slowed and finally ground to a stop. Smiles and sly grins disappeared from the faces of the customers. Dusty's mouth closed as he looked at Carl's angry expression. Barry looked up and scrunched his face.

"We're just havin' a little fun," Dusty said in explanation.

"The show's over, folks," Carl said. "The boy here isn't dancing anymore."

Chapter 7

It was Labor Day, 1974. Carl took the day off even though he had ground to till. He knew that he should try to spend some time with Barry before he returned him to St. Vincents in a few days. For some strange reason he had a feeling of dread.

Joan opened the wicker picnic basket and brought out a covered dish of fried chicken. She peeked beneath the aluminum wrap and inhaled the aroma. Pulling a plastic lid off of a container of potato salad, she placed it on the blanket. She looked around at people milling about the lake. It was a balmy day for September.

As Joan set the array of dishes and silverware about, her mind roamed over the past weeks. It really hadn't been that bad having Barry around. Of course, he wasn't their idea of what a son should be. He was a complete antithesis of Ricky.

Barry was a twelve-year-old with the intelligence of a four-year-old. Some days, Joan thought, his mind seemed less responsive than others. She remembered how clumsily he had buttered his toast at breakfast, finally knocking over his milk. She smiled to herself recalling how he looked up at her, grimaced, and stuck out his tongue. She remembered his determined attempts at wiping up the puddle of milk with a rag. At last, he handed the rag back to her with a proud grin on his face, the milk dripping all over the floor. Joan started to protest but instead kissed him on his bald head, only to be hugged back so tightly she gasped for breath.

Joan watched his deep concentration as he tried to figure out how to make his bed. She shook her head with a combination of humor, frustration, and pride as she looked at the muddle of wrinkled, lumpy blankets, one side drooping to the floor and the other side barely covering the edge of the mattress. Again, she praised his efforts. She knew she should take time to show him the proper way to make his bed, but knew the effort seemed wasted since he was returning to St. Vincents in a few days.

Joan thought back, hearing his exuberant and excited screams in her mind, to when their barnyard rooster chased him around the pen when he was helping her feed the chickens.

Joan turned, watching Carl bait a hook with a worm. A wave of revulsion swam through her, but Barry was jumping up and down with excitement. With a huge grin Carl watched as he cast the line only a few feet from the bank. Joan suddenly realized that was the happiest she had seen him since Ricky's death. Joan slapped her knee and giggled watching his attempts. Barry, however, watched and listened intently trying to absorb the detailed instructions on how to cast. It didn't matter to him if the line went out fifty feet or five feet, he was overjoyed. She recalled how Ricky, with a flick of his wrist, deftly sent his line far out into the lake last year. She cautioned herself for always comparing the two boys. They were and always would be as different as night and day.

Joan watched Carl hand Barry the pole gesturing the proper technique of casting. Carl's Italian heritage surfaced as arms and hands flew about in explanation. Shades of Mama Wadonelli, she thought, smiling.

Barry took hold of the pole and with a tremendous grunt swung the line over his head. The cork fell at his feet, not reaching the water. The second and third times produced a snarl of intricate tangles. On the fourth trial, Carl ducked just in time as the line whirled dangerously close to his head. The hook finally landed, embedded in the front of his shirt.

Joan pleasantly noticed that there was no tone of anger in Carl's muffled, distant voice. He merely repeated the instructions while he dislodged the hook. Finally, Barry managed to place the line ten feet from the bank. Carl heaped praise on him and patted his bald head. Barry looked up and grinned proudly.

Finally, Carl walked up the bank, his face flushed with exertion, and dropped down beside Joan on the blanket.

"Keep your eye on that red cork, Joan," he instructed. "If it disappears, let me know and I'll run down and help the kid."

Joan looked out toward the lake and at Barry's squat body. His eyes were riveted to the dancing cork only a few feet from the bank.

"It's almost too close to the bank to catch fish, isn't it?" she asked.

Carl shook his head. "Oh, no, there's fish there. Not real big ones like farther out, but there's some there." He smiled. "Don't you remember, a year ago, that nice yellow cat Rick caught? It must've weighed a couple pounds."

"Yes, but his line was much farther out than Barry's." She nipped the edge of her tongue in self-reproach. There she was comparing the two boys again. "It took a lot of casts for him to finally catch on, didn't it?"

"Well, he's never fished before. Any kid would have trouble if it was his first time."

Joan smiled and nodded. "Yeah, I suppose so." She watched Barry stand poised, watching every movement of the cork. "Even from the back you can tell he isn't right, can't you?"

Carl cocked his head to one side and watched Barry for a few moments. "I don't think he looks so bad. He's kind of short and sort of dumpy ..."

"... and sort of bald and sort of fat and sort of slant-eyed and sort of retarded," she added.

Carl turned with a scowl. "Give the kid a break, Joan! Give the kid a break!"

Joan looked at him, puzzled, but said nothing.

Carl clasped his hands behind his head, propped himself against a tree, and closed his eyes allowing the sun that sifted through the branches to coat his face. "He tries hard. Why would God do that to a poor kid? He can't do anything the way he should. And everything he can do takes such effort ... such concentration. It isn't fair that He should give such a dirty deal to a kid."

"Remember what you said a few months ago. You said God doesn't do anything to anyone. It just happens. We all have free will." Joan watched Carl's face grow intent as he talked about Barry. She knew it hurt him.

Joan looked at Barry. He jumped up and down with excitement. Joan visored her eyes. "Carl! Carl, hurry! I don't see the cork. I think he's got a bite!"

Carl's eyes popped open. With a grunt, he pushed himself to his feet and ran faster than Joan had seen him run in years. Barry clutched the pole in both hands. Joan craned her neck to see.

Carl placed his large hands on Barry's hands and together they lifted the line out of the water. A little sun perch wiggled on the end of the line. Barry ran to retrieve the flopping fish. After several attempts trying to trap the slick creature, he held it up with a huge, victorious grin on his face. Carl stood with his hands on his hips, nodding his head with approval.

"Joan," he yelled, "get down here with the camera! Hurry up!" He gestured. "I want you to take a picture of me and the kid … uh, of me and Barry."

Joan focused the camera on Carl standing with his arm proudly draped around Barry's shoulders. Barry held the fish up with pride. They both acted as though it was a seventy pound marlin, she thought. Joan asked them to move forward, backward, farther apart and then closer together before snapping the picture.

Carl sighed. "Now, Barry, what say you and me get some fried chicken. I'm starved."

Barry gnawed on the chicken leg eagerly. Carl replenished the food on his plate as soon as the bottom was visible.

"Carl, let the kid breathe, will you? He's going to explode," Joan said, laughing.

"A guy works up a big appetite out-of-doors, fishing," he said, prodding Barry with his elbow.

Barry looked up, his lips coated with chicken breading.

"Listen, kid," Carl said, gesturing. "I'm going to take you to a real big lake someday. Not a little city lake like this one. You should see the walleye and bass at Neosha Lake. Some of 'em go ten, twenty pounds. And boy, do they fight. They can pull you right out of the boat."

Barry continued eating seeming not to comprehend.

"You know, Barry, there's nothing like camping out in the night air and getting up at the crack of dawn to fish. It makes you feel great. It makes you feel like a real man." He pushed Barry playfully.

Barry wobbled one way and then another and finally became completely unbalanced and toppled over on his back, giggling. Carl rolled him over, tickling him in the stomach. Barry tried to roll away and Carl went after him. Joan smiled to herself without realizing it.

"Carl, let him up. You're going to tickle him to death," she cheerfully warned.

Barry giggled in his graveled voice. Carl hovered over him, still probing his ribs. Barry wiggled out from under and pounced on Carl with a yell. Carl feigned defeat as Joan clapped her hands. Tears of hilarity rolled down Carl's cheeks. On his back, Carl looked up at Barry's grinning face. Looking back down at him were two pairs of slanted eyes. A girl who looked exactly like Barry, except for her two neatly woven red braids, grinned down at him.

Carl sat up with Barry in his lap. The girl clapped her hands and started digging her fingers in Carl's mid-section. Carl looked around, feeling embarrassed, trying to find the person who this little girl belonged to. A middle-aged woman with grayish-streaked hair came running from a park bench to grab the girl's arm.

"Amy! What are you doing? Let these people alone." The woman looked at Carl and Joan and smiled warmly. "I"m terribly sorry. Amy knows no strangers. Someday, it's going to get her into trouble." She extended her hand to Joan. "My name is Nelda Bertrand and this is my daughter, Amy, whom you've already met. We live in Stockton."

Joan smiled and shook the woman's outstretched hand. "Oh, no. She didn't do anything wrong. My name is Joan Wadonelli and this is my husband, Carl."

The woman waited a moment, looking down at Barry. "And this young man?"

Carl raised Barry straight up in the air. Barry flailed his arms about, giggling. "This guy is Barry, Mrs. Bertrand. He's a number one fisherman and a pretty good wrestler, too."

Mrs. Bertrand nodded toward Amy. "Amy, meet Barry Wadonelli."

Carl and Joan looked at each other, shrugged, and smiled.

"Shake Barry's hand, Amy," Mrs. Bertrand instructed.

Amy jutted her hand out and pumped Barry's hand heartily. Her deep voice replicated Barry's. "Hi, Barry. I'm Amy Bertrand and I'm in the Trainable Level II class at Green Oaks. Mrs. Marshall is my teacher. I'm twelve years old. We are learning how to set the table and make our beds this week. The other day, Clarrisa Mosley brought her pet hamster, Fred, to our ..."

Mrs. Bertrand chuckled and shook her head. "Okay, Amy, I think Barry gets the idea."

Amy smiled and grimaced. Joan couldn't get over the resemblance of the two children. Amy had the same small round head, flat face, rounded shoulders and gutteral voice. She walked with a hunched gait and grimaced just like Barry.

Amy looked down at the plate of fried chicken setting on the blanket and pointed. "Can I have that chicken leg?"

Mrs. Bertrand jerked her arm with stern reproach. "Amy! You know better than that. You always wait until someone invites you to have some. You never ask!"

Joan took the plate of chicken and offered it to Amy. "That's okay. We've got more than we can eat. Carl's been stuffing Barry. Would you like a piece, Amy?"

Amy looked up at her mother and grimaced.

"Go ahead and take a piece and be sure to thank the lady," Mrs. Bertrand reminded her.

Amy took a piece of chicken and smiled. "Yum! Thank you Mrs ... Mrs ..."

"Wadonelli," Joan told her.

"Mrs. Wad ... Mrs. Wad ... "

"Call her Mrs. Wadi, Amy," Carl said, laughing. "That's a lot easier."

"Mrs. Wadi," Amy said.

Barry and Amy laughed together and clapped their hands.

Barry reached out and took Amy's hand. "Come on," he said, "let's go fish. I already caught one. It's down by the water." He pointed toward the lake. "Do you want to go see it?"

Amy turned and looked up at her mother once again. Mrs. Bertrand nodded and Amy turned to Barry and nodded.

They walked, hand in hand, down to the lake with Amy's braids bouncing.

Joan looked at Mrs. Bertrand. "I can't get over it. They look like twins."

Carl nodded in agreement.

"I'm sorry, but I think I'm confused. You are the parents of the boy, aren't you?" Mrs. Bertrand asked.

Joan shook her head. "No. My husband and I are just taking care of Barry for a month. His mother was killed in an auto accident several weeks ago."

Mrs. Bertrand covered her mouth. "How tragic. I'm sorry to hear that."

Joan felt very comfortable with this woman.

Carl rose to his feet and walked over to the women. "You see, ma'm, we sort of got cornered into taking care of the kid for a month by a nun at Catholic Charities." He hunched his shoulders in a gesture of acceptance. "It's a long story. But the short of it is, we lost our only child five months ago. So about a month ago we went to Catholic Charities with the intention of seeing if we could adopt a baby. Instead, we came home with a twelve-year-old mentally handicapped kid."

Mrs. Bertrand looked out toward the lake where Barry was proudly displaying a stiff sun perch to an admiring Amy. "Oh, you will never regret it, Mr. Wadonelli. It's like ..." She thought for a moment. "... it's like an insurance to always have sunshine every day for the rest of your lives. I think it's wonderful of you to adopt Barry. But, believe me, you folks are the lucky ones."

Joan's brows furrowed. "Wait a minute, Mrs. Bertrand. We're not going to adopt him. We just brought him home for a month so he could get out of the place for awhile. Next Monday, back he goes to St. Vincents. We're not getting tied to a mentally handicapped kid for the rest of our lives. Not after we've had a child like Ricky."

Mrs. Bertrand's smile faded.

"Oh, Mrs. Bertrand, I'm so sorry," Joan said, cringing. "That was really insensitive of me."

Mrs. Bertrand raised her hand in understanding. "That's alright, Mrs. Wadonelli. I understand. To people who have not been around Down Syndrome children, it would seem like a terrible burden, I'm sure. And, at times, it is. Everything they do takes more time, patience, energy, and frustration. But once they learn it, it's the greatest reward for them and for you."

"Why do you suppose this has happened to these poor kids?" Carl asked. "It isn't fair that they have to go through life with ... with such a handicap."

Mrs. Bertrand smiled with a faraway look in her eyes. "Mr. Wadonelli, these are God's chosen few. They are all happy and free of worry." She nodded toward the children. "Look at them out there. They are serenely content. They have few inhibitions. If they want you to be their friend, they just come up and ask you. And when they do this, they have no devious motives. The Down Syndrome adults and children I've seen are carefree and cheerful most of the time. They are very affectionate and easily amused. They love life, beauty, and music."

Carl shaded his eyes, looking toward the lake. "I never thought of it that way before."

"They don't worry about taxes or the spiraling inflation or the energy crisis or the impending wars in the world. Their minds are free of the clutter of modern civilization. They don't even worry where their next meal is coming from or where they will sleep. They know someone will take care of them. And they don't worry about death."

Joan winced and rubbed her bare arms. "Oh, I should hope not. No child should have to worry about that."

Mrs. Bertrand smiled. "Death is an ever-present threat to a Down Syndrome child. These children are susceptible to many illnesses and do not live to a normal person's life expectancy, usually. Leukemia, heart trouble, respiratory ailments, and other illnesses are more likely to occur to these children than the normal child."

"But why do the two of them look so much alike? They look like they could be brother and sister," Joan said.

"All Down Syndrome children have somewhat the same physical features. They're stunted in growth and have a small, round head with a flat face. Their eyes sort of squint." She smiled. "Thus, giving them the name, 'mongoloid' because their eyes resemble the Asian race. The ears are misshapened, the nose is stubby, and the tongue is large and flabby with fissures. They have thin hair, sometimes none like Barry. And there are other less obvious physical features that they all share. Many of them grimace."

"What causes it, Mrs. Bertrand?" Carl asked with interest.

"Well, it's a chromosome abnormality. It gets pretty technical and I don't understand it exactly. All I know is that most of these children tend to be born at the end of large families. It seems also to be related to the age of the mother. The risk of giving birth to a child with Down Syndrome rises with the age of the mother. Amy, for instance, came along when I had my other three children raised and in college."

Joan winced and shook her head. "How terrible for you."

Mrs. Bertrand laughed and shook her head. "Not at all, Mrs. Wadonelli. Like I said, she's sunshine insurance for me each and every day. She gives my husband and me so much happiness and pleasure. God was very good to us." She closed her eyes for a moment in thought. "That's not to say it's easy all of the time. You must be fair and firm with them. They are like any child and will throw temper tantrums, refuse to try, lounge about letting you wait on them, and refuse to accomplish what they are able to if you allow it. If you expect little from them, they will reward you with little, just like any normal child."

"Then Amy goes to school?" Carl asked.

"Yes, she goes to a special education class every day. I'm sure Barry must have attended one also since he looks so well behaved and socially adjusted. Someone has trained him well. Amy has learned so much, and, of course, we continue the self-help skills, speech, socialization, and prevocational development at home."

Joan turned to Carl. "We didn't even ask about schooling."

"Well, it really doesn't matter," Carl said. "He'll be going back in a few days anyway."

Mrs. Bertrand smiled to herself and nodded. "I understand how you feel, but when you return him, life will not be the same for you. You'll be giving back one of God's chosen children."

Suddenly, a scream came from across the lake. Mrs. Bertrand covered her mouth. Amy had stumbled on a rock and had fallen head first into the lake. The two of them had wandered to the opposite side of the lake and were almost out of view.

Joan froze. Scenes of that horrible day in April flashed through her mind. "Carl, do something! The little girl fell in the lake! It's deep on that side; that's where they boat!"

Carl charged forward. Punctuated grunts of exertion exploded from his gaping mouth. As he ran, he shaded his eyes and looked to the opposite side of the lake. Amy was nowhere to be seen in the water. Carl stopped in his tracks and gasped as he watched Barry jump into the lake feet first.

"God, no!" he shouted. "Barry, no ... no, don't! You'll both drown. Barry ... son. Oh, God!"

Carl watched as Barry disappeared beneath the water.

Crowds of people ran toward the lake to try to aid the children.

Carl darted forward praying beneath his breath. "God in heaven, don't let it happen again. Save Barry and Amy and I'll never ask for anything again. Please save both of them ... please."

Carl pushed his way through the spectators and peered into the deep, murky water. He searched the surface for some sight of either of them. His heart pounded in his chest. Tears welled in his eyes as he mumbled prayers he said as a kid ... a good Catholic kid.

Leaning forward, he saw a shiny bald head slowly rise to the water's surface. Barry threw his head back spewing water from his gaping mouth. Carl reached out catching him by the shirt and dragged him up on the boat dock.

Looking down, Carl breathed a sigh of relief. Barry had one of Amy's skimpy red, braids clutched in his fist. Carl and a few men crowding the dock, jumped in and hauled both children out of the water. Barry gasped for breath, water dripping from his nose and mouth. Amy vomited and gagged. But, both of them were very much alive.

Everyone stood back as Carl grabbed Barry and held him to him. Barry looked around at the crowd and grimaced. The spectators applauded. Carl held Barry and thanked God beneath his breath.

Mrs. Bertrand knelt beside Amy smoothing back her wet bangs. She looked up and touched Barry's pudgy hand. "Thank you, Barry," she said, her voice shaking. "You are truly one of God's chosen children."

Chapter 8

Sister Angelica adjusted her glasses and tried her best to smile. "Well, Barry, it's good to have you back. We've missed you. Sister Mary Joseph has been beside herself without you."

Barry looked up and grimaced.

"Did you have a nice time with Mr. and Mrs. Wadonelli?" she asked.

Barry looked at Carl and nodded. "I like Mr. Wadi." Barry encircled Carl's waist and squeezed hard.

"We got a real kick out of having him, Sister. Joan ... she couldn't come to bring him back. She had a lot of things to do around the house. I've got to get right back and get to the field," Carl stammered.

"I understand, Mr. Wadonelli." Sister Angelica looked down at Barry with his small suitcase setting at his feet. She patted his head with affection. Walking to her desk, she pressed a button on her inter-com and summoned Sister Mary Joseph. "Sister will be here presently to take you to your room, Barry. Did you remember to get all of your things?"

Barry nodded and pointed at the suitcase.

Carl shifted uneasily from one foot to the other.

Sister Angelica gestured politely. "Please, Mr. Wadonelli, sit down."

"No, no," Carl answered. "That's all right. I'd just as soon stand."

The door swung wide and Sister Mary Joseph ran toward Barry, sweeping him into her arms. Barry embraced her with affection. "Well," she said, "you look healthy and well fed. And I do believe you've grown a full inch in just a month," she teased.

Barry stood straight and rigid with his arms glued to his sides.

"Is Barry ready to go to his room, Sister?" Sister Mary Joseph asked.

"Yes, please." She paused and glanced at Carl. "Barry, shake Mr. Wadonelli's hand and thank him for giving you such a nice time this past month."

Barry's hand jutted forward and clutched Carl's. He pumped it vigorously. "Thank you, Mr. Wadi."

Carl's eyes glazed for a moment. He cleared his throat and fought for composure. "We had quite a time, didn't we, kid? I'll … I'll always remember it. And I'll come and get you one of these days and you and I will go bass fishin' up at Neosha Lake."

Barry smiled .

Sister Mary Joseph took Barry's suitcase and led him toward the door. Barry followed along until he got to the door and then stopped and turned and looked back at Carl. Abruptly, he pulled away from Sister Mary Joseph's clasp and ran toward him to give him one last hug around the waist.

Sister Angelica snorted into her handkerchief and made the sign of the cross.

Carl looked down and kissed Barry's hairless head. Barry turned and ran back to Sister Mary Joseph and they both disappeared through the door.

Sister Angelica fondled her cross. "Well, Mr. Wadonelli, I want to thank you and Mrs. Wadonelli so much. You took him home when he needed to get away from here. You kept your bargain and the Lord and I will keep ours."

A solemn look came to Carl's face. "You know he's quite a kid, Sister. I'll bet there isn't one kid in a hundred quite like Barry." He chuckled to himself. "Oh, he's a little slow and clumsy, but he makes up for it in guts and effort."

Sister Angelica nodded and smiled.

"The first night he was with us I think he was a little scared, but after that he warmed right up. Damndest thing I ever saw."

Carl pressed his fingers to his lips. "Sorry, Sister. I didn't mean to say that."

"That's all right, Mr. Wadonelli, I understand."

"He went with me everywhere. Out to milk the cows, to the field … everywhere. One day I took him to a little cafe I always go to in Lawton. He broke a whole stack of dishes, but it wasn't his fault. The dishwasher had them stacked too high. He helped Joan feed the chickens and gather the eggs. An old cantankerous rooster chased him all over the pen." He laughed awkwardly.

Sister Angelica tried to chuckle, but ended up nodding.

"He was quite a spiller at home. But, he always tried to clean up the messes he made. One morning, he got dressed and brushed his teeth in only twenty minutes and he even got his shoestrings tied pretty well, too."

"It sounds like he did just fine with you and Mrs. Wadonelli," Sister Angelica acknowledged.

"He did at that, Sister." Carl poked a cigarette in his mouth and lit it. "If this bothers you, tell me Sister, and I'll put it out."

"Oh, no. I like the smell of it." Sister Angelica leaned toward Carl in confidence. "To be perfectly honest with you, it makes me want one. I used to smoke before I entered the convent, God forgive me."

Carl pointed at her and laughed. "You did? You really did?" He shook his head. "You know, for some reason that doesn't surprise me. Anyone who could put a hammerlock on me with one arm while she takes her foot and braces it against the door has done some street fighting in her day."

Sister Angelica tried to muffle her laughter by placing her hand over her mouth, but it still came out loud and robust. "I had five brothers to contend with. They taught me how to fight and how to smoke I might add. You won't tell on me, will you, Mr. Wadonelli? Everyone around here thinks I've always been a perfect saint."

Carl reached out and shook her hand. "Your secret is safe with me, Sister."

"Thank you, Mr. Wadonelli."

A long uncomfortable pause took over .

"Well, I suppose you're busy and like I said I need to get back to the field," Carl said.

"I have plenty of time, Mr. Wadonelli … plenty of time."

Carl extended his hand and it was warmly received. "Sorry, Sister that we couldn't do business."

"The Lord and I haven't given up yet, Mr. Wadonelli."

"You know, Barry is quite a fisherman once he got the hang of it. He caught himself a nice little sun perch. He was grinning from ear to ear."

Sister Angelica nodded eagerly.

Carl turned to leave but stopped in mid-stride and looked around. "Oh, the big event of the visit was when he saved a little girl's life. She would've drowned if it hadn't been for Barry's quick thinking."

Sister Angelica clutched her cross in anticipation. "What did you just say, Mr. Wadonelli? Please sit down and tell me more." She motioned toward a chair.

Carl walked back and slowly sank into the large, leather overstuffed chair. He leaned forward. "Well, this lady, Mrs. Bertrand, said that he was really one of God's chosen children …"

Joan ran the dustcloth over the coffee table, and rearranged the figurines and doilies. She just realized that it was the third time she had done it in the past hour. She looked down at the water stain where Barry had placed a glass, forgetting to use his coaster. She and Carl had had that coffee table for ten years and had never put a scratch on it. And Ricky had always been so careful. This kid comes for a month and mars if forever, she thought.

Joan told herself to get up and sort clothes for the laundry. The kid had put her behind on her washing and ironing. He was always wetting the bed. She had to wash the bedding practically

82

every day. It would be so much less work without him. No more spilled milk, no jelly on the carpet, no mattresses smelling of urine, no bedding half-on, half-off the bed, no more broken dishes. He was gone and she was glad, she thought, nodding her head.

She and Carl did not need someone like him to complicate their lives. It would be good to be independent. It was a silly pipe dream. They weren't meant to have any more children. And certainly not a twelve year old mentally handicapped kid. Joan told herself that she was relieved he was gone. Now they could get back to their routine and their adjustment to living without Ricky.

Joan lowered herself into the divan and stroked Pete lounging at her feet. A lump under the divan cushion caused her to get up and pull the cushion out. There, squashed in a corner of lint and lost coins, was Barry's stuffed dog, Toto, one ear hanging limply fastened with a safety pin. Joan picked the pitiful looking toy up and pressed it to her face. Streams of tears ran down her cheeks.

The door opened and she turned her back so Carl would not see her. Hurriedly, she brushed the tears away before he entered the room. Suddenly, a pair of short, pudgy arms went around her waist and shut off her breath. She looked in the doorway to find Carl standing there grinning from ear to ear. Barry looked up at her and grimaced. Pete got up and waddled toward Barry, his short tail wagging frantically.

Chapter 9

"Mama, do you want me to put more garlic in the meatballs?" Leona May picked up a chunk of raw hamburger and munched on it. Her eyes rolled back in her head as she savored the taste. "I think it needs a little more." She cut little chunks of garlic with swift motions of a well-sharpened knife and sprinkled it over the frying hamburger.

Lonnie Frank bounded into the kitchen, stepping in Mama's cat bowl. Milk and Kitty Delights ran in a pool on the flowered linoleum.

Mama clutched her head with both hands. "God in heaven, that boy could make a good Christian swear. Look at Immaculata's cat bowl all empty. She won't get her dinner tonight. Leona May, can't you and that husband of yours train those children?"

Leona May sucked the inside of her cheek with agitation and placed her hands on her large hips. "Lonnie Frank, for shame! Slow yourself down or you'll bust a gut. Look at that mess you made for Grandmama."

Mama winced and wiped between her first and second chins. "It isn't a mess for Mama; it's a mess for Leona May. There's a rag below the dishtowel drawer."

"Well, Mama, you know what I mean," Leona May whined. "I'll clean it up … I'll clean it up."

Mama stiffened and furrowed her dark brows. "Don't get testy with me, Leona May. I'm still your Grandmama and you're never too old to scold."

"Oh, Mama, I know it." Leona May rushed over and gave her an affectionate hug. "I didn't mean anything, for heaven's sake."

She patted Mama on the shoulder.

Herbie Jr. entered the kitchen dragging Immaculata by the tail. The cat clawed at the slick linoleum in desperation as it howled in agony.

Mama crossed herself and grabbed Immaculata from Herbie Jr. "What has that little heathen done to you?" she asked, smoothing its fur. "It's a wonder you have a hair left on your body with these kids in the house." She turned to Leona May. "You know, Leona May, that Immaculata usually spends all of her time under the bed or couch when your bambinos are around. Last time you came she had diarrhea for a week. Do you know what it's like to clean up after a cat with diarrhea?" Mama fanned herself with her hanky. "Let me tell you, Mama was praying to the Lord for strength. I walked around with a mop trailing that cat for a whole week after your last visit."

"Oh, Mama, my kids never caused that. It probably was something going around." Leona May thought for a moment. "Maybe some cat flu or something."

Donna Marie toddled in with her diaper hanging below her bare buttocks. She sat down in the milk and Kitty Delights with glee.

Mama screamed and reached for Heaven. "Blessed Mary, help me tonight." She pointed. "Look, Leona May, Donna Marie is sopping up the milk and Kitty Delights with her diaper. Call that husband of yours in to help you with these children before they drive Mama to drink!"

Leona May's nasal voice shrieked for assistance. "Herbie! Herbie ... for crying outloud! Get in here and help me with these kids!"

Mama wiped between her second and third chins in exasperation. "That husband of yours, Leona May, he's not worth his salt. He doesn't belong to any church. He's gone all the time on the road. He's not even a decent father."

Herbie hurried into the kitchen with Little Joey in one arm and Edith Ann in the other. A look of dread came to his face when he saw Mama's stern stare.

"Look at him, Leona May. In the parlor resting while you run your poor self to a frazzle taking care of these children."

Little Joey held a crocheted doily in his sticky hands.

"Get that doily away from him. Aunt Fellona gave that to me fifty years ago. She brought it over from the old country."

Actually, Mama had bought it three years ago at Woolworth's.

Leona May snatched it away before Mama had a chance to see that Little Joey had wiped his nose on it as well.

Herbie presented Edith Ann to Leona May. "Here," he said, "she just messed in her pants."

Leona May breathed a deep sigh and took Edith Ann to the bathroom to change her.

Herbie stood there, shifting from one foot to the other. "Been hot for September, huh, Mama?"

Mama turned to him and squinted her little pig eyes with vengeance. "Hot! You don't know hot until you enter the gates of hell. That's where you're going. Mama asked you nicely on your last visit if you were ready to join some church. I didn't insist that it would be our church. You said you were thinking about it. You have had time to think about it." She placed her hands on her full hips. "Now, what is your answer? Are you going to join the saintly ones above in a garden paradise floating majestically about with huge white wings now and then touching your toes to golden streets, chanting beautiful prayers of thanks, feeling so light and pure and lovely, listening to choirs of angels in a chorus of holy anthems … " Mama paused and licked her upper lip. " … or are you going to shovel coal for eternity?"

Little Joey pulled at his dad's hand, wanting his freedom.

Mama stood there, glaring her warning. She shrugged. "It's your soul. It's not mine. I know where I'm going. I was fortunate, I suppose, to have parents who were concerned about my soul. Again, I am not asking you to join our church, but I am asking you to join some church."

Herbie squirmed about, still clutching Little Joey's out-stretched hand. Little Joey wiggled loose and reached for a piece of garlic bread. Mama slapped him smartly with a flyswatter and he withdrew his hand quickly sucking his battered fingers.

"Mama … Mama …" Herbie stammered, "I … I … did somethin' this week."

Mama tapped an impatient toe and narrowed her eyes. "May Jesus have guided you this last week. May Papa in Heaven have guided you this week. May every spirit of every good person have guided you this week. May every …"

"Mama!" Herbie slapped his mouth realizing how loud he had shouted. He lowered his voice immediately. "Mama … I went and saw Father Mulhaney last Wednesday. I … I'm starting instructions tomorrow."

Mama pulled her hanky out of her tight sleeve and patted her forehead. Deep breaths came from her gaping mouth. Beads of perspiration popped out on her upper lip.

Herbie rushed to her and supported her as her legs started to tremble and then buckle. He grunted under her ponderous weight.

"Leona May! Come quick! Mama is about ready to faint!" Herbie groaned as Mama allowed him to support all of her weight. "Hurry, Leona May … give me a hand!"

Leona May came rushing out of the bathroom dragging a naked Edith Ann by the hand.

"My god, Herbie! What did you do to her?"

Mama grasped Herbie's shoulder and eased herself into a kitchen chair. It shook under her weight. "No … no, Mama is all right. Mama is glorious!" She stuck her hanky down into the cleft of her bosom. "Leona May, God is good. God has guided your husband. Praise God! Now, I can die with a smile on my face. Now, I can look down from Heaven with Papa and be proud of my family still here on earth." She made the sign of the cross. "Praise Jesus!"

Leona May hugged Mama and sniffled with happiness. "Isn't it wonderful, Mama. I was going to tell everybody as soon as Carl and Joan got here. And the great thing about it is, he did it on his own. He did it on his own free will."

Mama pulled back with a disgruntled look on her face. "Certainly no one forced him!" She instantly mellowed. "Herbert, now I can call you my son-in-law. Now, I can treat you like a ... like a ..."

"Human," Herbie offered.

"Whatever," Mama assured him. Mama blew her nose with a loud honk. "Mama's prayers are being answered too fast for Mama to bear. Herbert is starting instructions. And my grand-son, Carl and his wife Joan calls and tells me that they are going to have another child. God is doing too much for Mama. Mama feels guilty with all of these prayers being granted all at once."

The doorbell rang and Lonnie Frank ran to open it. "Leona May, see if the spaget sauce has simmered long enough. That has to be my Carl."

Lonnie Frank bolted into the kitchen. "Hey, Grandmama, Uncle Carl and Aunt Joan are here and they have a funny lookin' kid with 'em."

Carl and Joan entered the kitchen self-consciously with Barry between them. They stood at the entrance for a moment, allowing everyone to absorb their presence. Mama pushed her huge body off the chair and walked to Carl to embrace him. She gave Joan a quick peck on the cheek. Finally, she looked down at Barry who returned her stare. He grimaced and stuck out his cracked tongue. Mama looked at Carl and then at Joan for an explanation. Leona May stood there without a word.

Carl cleared his throat as though he were preparing a pre-sentation. "Mama, Leona May ... and Herbie, we'd like you to meet our new son ... Barry."

Mama looked doubtfully at Carl and then at Joan's nervous face. She then lowered her body to a chair clutching her breast.

###

Everyone but Carl and Joan watched Barry eat his spaghetti. Mama eyed him with suspicion.

Barry's teeth ground together as he chewed his meal. Strands of spaghetti peeked out of his lips and he pushed them back in with his hand continuing to eat. He looked around, smiling and grimacing. Leona May looked down at her plate. Barry wiped his mouth with his napkin and folded his hands in his lap.

Lonnie Frank eyed Barry curiously. "Ma, why does he eat so funny?" he asked.

Leona May poked him with her elbow. "Be quiet or I'll take you out to the kitchen."

The usual animated conversation was absent. Joan ladled another spoonful of sauce onto Barry's spaghetti and he looked up and smiled.

Mama eyed his clumsy attempts at getting the spoon to his mouth. She saw his thick, cracked tongue lick the spoon and she pushed her chair back pressing her palm to her quivering lips.

Carl's appetite deserted him. He nibbled at his pasta and shuffled his salad around on his plate. At last, Barry was finished. Barry wiped his mouth with his napkin and folded his hands in his lap once again.

"Lonnie Frank," Carl said, "would you take Barry to the other room to play?"

Lonnie Frank looked at his mother for approval. Leona May nodded and he motioned for Barry to follow him to the living room.

Mama waited until both boys had left. Then her arms vaulted toward the ceiling. "My Lord! Tell Mama that it's just a bad dream. Let Mama wake up and have it … him … gone!"

Leona May screwed up her face and stared at Carl. "If this is your idea of a joke, let me tell you, it's a pretty poor one."

"I think he seems like a nice kid," Herbie interjected.

Carl hit his plate with a spoon. "Now, listen to me. It isn't a joke. We are adopting Barry. He's a great kid. He needs parents and we need a son."

Mama fanned herself with an old Biblical fan. "I can barely speak. How could you do this? And after having a son so beautiful … so pure … so perfect … God's angel?"

"Carl," Leona May said in a whisper, "how could you do this to Mama? Don't you know that kid will be Mama's Great Grandson. Mama's been praying all these months for you to have a child … but not one of those!"

Mama wiped her temple and between her first and second chins. She raised her hand and all attention was relinquished to her.

"Mama wants to speak," she said. "When Mama prayed all of these months for you to have a bambino, I meant one of your very own flesh and blood. I meant a little dark-eyed bambino, one that Papa and I could be proud of, one who would be baptized in our Holy Church and take his first communion in your parish Church and years later Confirmation, one who would pray to our savior and know in his heart what he is praying for. I prayed to Jesus every night for five months." Mama clasped her hands together and motioned toward Heaven. "And then it seemed Mama's prayers were being answered right and left. Herbert has seen the heavenly light and is joining our faith, a little late and his soul is no doubt a little tarnished, but, nevertheless, he has been persuaded by our Lord." She paused and wiped the spittle that gathered in the corners of her mouth. "And before that I get a call that my grandson Carl and his wife, Joan, will have a child. Naturally, Mama thought God had brought forth another miracle and Joan would have her own in a few months." Mama beat upon her heavy bosom and looked skyward. "Well, I can tell you I was sure that Jesus and His Mother Mary must be favoring Mama these days. I was sure Papa was weeping in Heaven with happiness. Mama is a tolerant woman … perhaps not a smart one … but a tolerant one. All of my children have bambinos whose eyes follow their head. Perhaps some are a bit irreverent and pesky, but they all know that they exist and it's up to their parents to teach them the Christian way." Mama licked the perspiration off her upper lip. "This boy, that you bring into Mama's house, is not all there. He gets up in the morning without purpose. He goes to bed at night without accomplishment. He will never know or understand our Lord. Mama cannot and will not accept this."

Joan looked at Leona May and then at Mama. "What does

91

this mean? Are you saying that Barry is not welcome in your home?"

Mama nodded. "When I prayed all of these months for you to have a bambino, Jesus did not answer me by sending you this." She pointed toward the living room.

Herbie threw his fork down, hitting his plate and chipping it. Mama squealed.

"Wait a minute … wait a minute! This kid is just a boy who doesn't have it altogether. He was polite and acted real nice at supper. I don't see why he's not welcome in this family just like anyone else." Herbie eyed Mama with a look of disdain. "You talk to me about needin' to see the light. I think you and Leona May could use some of that light. All of your prayin' hasn't made you such good Christians."

Mama clutched her breast in agony. She reached for Heaven. "No, Papa, please tell me I didn't hear it. Someone is questioning Mama's Christian ethics. Sweet Jesus! How much can Mama stand?"

Leona May stood up and stomped over to Herbie. "You be quiet! Don't you see you're upsettin' Mama?"

A calm look came to Herbie's homely face. "Maybe it's time she was upset. Father Mulhaney told me the other day that it's the way you act and the Christian things you do that make you a good person and one of God's flock. And I believe him."

Mama sniffled into her hanky. "Oh, Jesus, why did you ordain those young, liberal priests. I cry that Vatican II ever happened."

Leona May stared at Herbie, nose-to-nose. "How dare you say those things to Mama?"

Herbie stood up calmly facing Mama and Leona May. His voice was forceful and deep. "I was going for my instructions tomorrow mostly because of her. But the way she's acting now, wild horses couldn't drag me over there. I'll stay what I am!"

Mama dropped her head into her hands. "Sweet Jesus! The boy has strayed before he was even in the fold! The Heavens are crashing down on Mama's head. I feel like I will soon be at Papa's side for my heart is bleeding in pain."

Carl got up and pointed at Mama. "You're as strong as a bull, Mama. You'll outlive all of us. But, let me tell you this, these monthly dinners are over for Joan and me if our son isn't welcome."

Barry walked into the dining room, carefully carrying Immaculata. A contented, deep purr came from the sleeping cat.

Mama snatched Immaculata away from Barry and held it to her bosom protectively.

Barry looked up at her, grimaced, and stuck out his tongue. Mama recoiled and squeezed Immaculata until she howled in pain. "Get this ... this ill-mannered boy out of Mama's house."

Carl attempted an explanation. "Mama, he just does that. He meant no disrespect." Carl met her cold, suspicious eyes. He threw up his hands. "Oh, what's the use? Come on, Joan, let's get out of here."

Barry ran over to Mama and hugged her with all of his strength. Mama sat there without movement or expression. Barry finally released her and ran toward the living room. Lonnie Frank stood behind the door and put his foot out as Barry approached. Barry stumbled over his foot and went sprawling onto the carpet. Lonnie Frank pointed his finger at Barry and laughed uproariously. Barry looked up at him from the floor and giggled. Lonnie Frank's wide grin changed quickly to a look of confusion.

Herbie grabbed Lonnie Frank by the arm and hit him smartly on the buttocks. The boy broke into tears and ran screaming to Leona May.

Joan guided Barry toward the door. Carl looked around at all of them grouped in the doorway. "I'll be seeing you, Herbie," he said.

As Carl closed the door behind him, he could hear Mama's piercing screams of anguish.

Chapter 10

Carl mentally went over the preparations for the night's poker game. He bought plenty of beer and snacks, a good sized chunk of summer sausage and cheese, and an economy size bag of pretzels. The table was set with an unopened deck of cards and Barry was separating the blue, red, and white chips into stacks. His thick tongue hung out of the corner of his mouth as he concentrated on making the stacks straight and even. A wave of pride swept through Carl as he watched his son. He liked the sound of it ..." his son."

Joan conveniently left for the evening to visit a friend. She always knew the appropriate time to be present and when to be absent, he thought. And poker nights were times to be absent. Carl assured himself that he was a lucky man to have such a wife ... and now a son, a son like Barry who brought sunshine into each day, just like Mrs. Bertrand had said. These past weeks had been like a wonderful dream, he thought.

Mama called only twice since that Sunday when she said Barry was not welcome in her home. Once she called to ask for the address of Cousin Angelina in Boston and the other time was to get Carl's advice for a holiday arrangement for Papa's grave. Neither time did she mention Barry.

Carl could not help but feel sad about this. He loved Mama. Afterall, what would he have done if she hadn't agreed to take care of him after his parents were killed? It had been hard on her. She had already raised her family. But, Mama was there for him. Carl realized that she was narrow in her beliefs and maneuvered and ruled the family with an iron, unyielding hand since

Papa died thirteen years ago. He remembered her unflinching faith throughout his childhood. Whenever anything went wrong, from not being chosen for a starting position on the baseball team to losing his best girl, she consoled him that it was God's will and He would take care of it. Carl knew that down deep she was a good woman ... a kind and forgiving woman. He just had to give her time, he thought. He knew that if Mama ever mellowed enough to get to know Barry, she would grow to love him just as they had. Carl placed his hand on Barry's shoulder and squeezed. Barry looked up and smiled.

Carl placed a bottle cap between his teeth and pried the bottle open with one downward thrust. Barry smiled watching the foam spew out of the neck of the bottle and splash to the floor. Tipping the bottle to his mouth, Carl allowed the beer to flow unhindered down his throat. Then he opened his mouth and let out a hollow, gusty belch. Barry clapped his hands and giggled.

"Daddy, Wadi ... give me some beer. First Mama gave Barry beer. Like beer better than pop."

Carl chuckled. "Your ma shouldn't give you beer. Beer isn't good for a kid. It'll make you stunted and you're already too short." He tickled Barry under the chin and he responded with a throaty giggle.

"Please, Daddy Wadi; I like beer."

Carl looked into Barry's pleading eyes. He felt his will yield. "Okay, but just a swallow ... no more," he warned.

Barry took the bottle and sipped it.

Carl set chairs around the kitchen table mentally counting the friends who had been invited. There was Ollie, Kebert, Lennie, Charley, and Dusty. At first he thought about not calling Dusty because of the incident a few weeks ago at the Blue Bird Cafe. Carl decided that he probably meant no harm. Yet, he knew that Dusty could be cruel at times. He enjoyed demeaning people.

Carl rehearsed how he would break the news about their adoption of Barry. Of course, the actual adoption would be months away after he and Joan had gone through a rigorous trial period. But, he felt they would have no trouble. He felt that it was he and Joan who had to measure up to Barry, certainly not the other way around. A loud belch from Barry interrupted his thoughts. Carl walked quickly over to him and snatched the empty beer bottle from his hand.

"There must've been a half bottle of beer there, kid. You shouldn't drink that much. If your mom finds out about this, she'll kill me."

A loud knock sounded at the door. Carl strode to the door and opened it greeting his friends. The sound of loud, male voices filled the room. Barry turned, somewhat startled with the sudden clamor.

Carl herded his buddies into the kitchen where everything was ready. The chips were ready. The beer and snacks were ready. And a new deck of cards, still in cellophane wrap, awaited.

Everyone was in a good mood, jostling each other and spicing their language with profanity. The noise subsided abruptly at the sight of Barry sitting and watching them enter the kitchen.

Dusty froze in mid-stride. He pointed. "Hey, that's the same kid you had at the Blue Bird a month ago. You still takin' care of him?" Dusty yelled over his shoulder. "Hey, guys, this is the kid I was tellin' you about that I saw with Wadonelli at the cafe last month. He must've broke twenty bucks worth of dishes that day."

Every eye went from Barry to Carl.

Carl walked to Barry and encircled his shoulders. His eyes got misty and his throat became tight. "Fellas, I want you to meet my new son ... Barry."

There was total silence for a moment until Charley Nelson lunged forward and grabbed Barry's hand. Barry pumped Charley's hand with exuberance. Everyone, except Dusty, waited in line to greet Barry. Barry grinned, feeling very important, but not understanding what all the commotion was about.

Dusty hit the table for order. "Just a minute ... just one minute! I think Wadonelli has some explaining to do. I thought you and Joan were just takin' care of the kid for a few weeks."

Ollie munched on a pretzel and shook his head. "Carl doesn't have to explain to anybody, Morton. He's got a kid and that's what's important. After losing Rick, if this makes him and Joan happy, that's all that matters."

Carl shook his head. "No, for once, Dusty's right. I should explain to you guys." He cleared his throat. "You see, Joan and I can't have any more kids." He shrugged. "Well, it would take a miracle for it to happen anyway. After losing Rick, we were very depressed for months. I was worried about her. Then she agreed to see Father Shawn. He convinced her to try Catholic Charities in Stockton. He said perhaps we could be foster parents or maybe even adopt a child." Carl studied each face. Everyone nodded in agreement except for Dusty. Dusty stood with his hands on his skinny hips with an expression of cynicism.

"Well, Joan and I decided to adopt a baby. But, we found that there was a long waiting list ... even three to four years. And besides, our ages were against us. Barry's mother had gotten killed out on Highway 67 the same week they received our application forms. The nun at St. Vincents persuaded us to take Barry home for a month to get him out of the place for awhile. It would be just a trial visit she said. We had no intention of keeping him. But, during that time, we got real close to him. I tried taking him back, but I couldn't. So, Joan and I decided to adopt him. It's the best decision we ever made." Carl paused for a moment and looked at Barry affectionately. "You see, fellas, our son is real special."

"Horse manure," Dusty exclaimed. "You just couldn't get a newborn so you had to accept the leftovers. Nobody wants to adopt those kind." He pointed at Barry.

One of Carl's heavy, black brows arched in warning. "Watch it, Dusty, or you'll find yourself outside with your keester up around your shoulders."

"You and who else?" Dusty dared.

Both men eyed each other with clenched fists.

"Hold on," Leonard pleaded, "we came here to have a good

time and play cards. I think it's great that Carl and Joan have a new kid. If they're happy, that's all that counts."

"That's right!" Kebert added.

Everyone, except for Dusty, reiterated his congratulations.

"It isn't any skin off of me if you want to raise a feeble-minded kid. You'll have him 'til he dies, you know that. He can't ever work or leave home. You and Joan are going to be saddled forever takin' care of him," Dusty said, shaking his head.

"Barry's just like other kids except he's slow. He goes to school. He likes to fish and play ball and everything. He's a great kid! But, you're probably right, Dusty, about him not ever living a normal life. For instance, he'll never get married and things like that. But some day, I think he'll be able to get a job. Of course, it'll have to be one that's fairly simple and routine, but that's alright. He's smart in certain ways and he tries real hard." Carl patted Barry's bald head. Barry looked up and grinned.

"Well, I'm just glad it's you instead of me," Dusty said, shaking his head. "Kids are a pain in the rear anyway, but one that isn't right in the head would be a double pain."

Ollie opened his buck-toothed mouth and expelled a high screech of laughter. "You act as though you're so smart, Morton. You haven't got any Ph.D. I wouldn't go around shaming people who aren't smart. As I remember it, back in grade school you were always at the bottom of the class. You even had trouble dustin' erasers."

"Stuff it, Ollie," Dusty retorted.

Everyone, including Barry, laughed.

"Hey, Carl," Charley said, "why don't you bring Barry over to the Cookie league game Saturday. It's been such nice fall weather, we're goin' to get a practice game in with the Bombers. He could sit on the bench and watch. Maybe even get to play, who knows? I'd bet he'd really enjoy it. My kid, Brian, plays shortstop. What do you say?"

Carl thought for a moment. "I should do some machinery repair. I'm way behind." He shrugged uncaringly. "What the heck, I can always do that. My son comes first. Barry and I will be there!"

"Great!" Charley bent over and looked Barry in the eye. "You like baseball, don't you kid?"

Barry grimaced. "I like baseball ... I like the New York Yankees ... I like Daddy Wadi and I like Mama Wadi and ..." he thought for a moment, "... and I like beer."

Everyone but Dusty roared with laughter.

Carl glowed with pride. He motioned. "Here, everyone, take your seats and let's get this show on the road."

Everyone scattered to pull out chairs and reach for snacks and drinks. Cigars and cigarettes were lit and top pants buttons were opened.

"First jack deals," Dusty announced as he wadded up the cellophane from the new deck of cards and threw it at Barry.

Barry's slow reaction didn't matter because the paper missed its intended mark. Barry looked at the wad of paper on the floor. Thinking it was a game, he slowly picked up the paper and threw it back at Dusty. It caught him directly on the tip of his long, beaked nose. This brought laughs from the group.

"Smart aleck kid. Doesn't know how to treat his elders. You can tell he's had no training," Dusty grumbled as he fingered his pencil-lead mustache.

The game started and Barry was forgotten as the smoke thickened, the empty beer bottles became numerous, and the swearing intensified. Barry moved about the table looking over everyone's shoulder. Sometimes he grabbed a half-drunk beer and a butt of a cigar and crawled beneath the table to finish both of them off. A player would reach for his cigar or his beer and discover them gone, only to feel too foolish to ask about them, thinking he had consumed one drink too many.

After many trips under the table, Barry had an increasingly more difficult time getting up. Many times he shared his booty with Pete who found it more and more difficult to stay awake.

Finally, the men called for a bathroom break, beer refills, and snacks. Barry walked to Carl and whispered in his ear.

"Can't the kid talk outloud? It isn't polite to whisper around company," Dusty said, accusingly. He was fifteen dollars behind and feeling especially surly.

"Barry said he wants to play cards, too," Carl said.

Every man laughed and elbowed each other.

"I play cards a long time ago when ... " He looked away a moment in concentration. "I watch other men ... I play sometimes."

Carl patted his head. "No, Barry, this is a grown-up man's game. The guys don't want any kids around."

"Besides, kid, it takes intelligence. You're a little short in that department." Dusty started to laugh, but sobered when he looked around at the stern faces of the others.

"Let him play one hand, Carl. Heck, it's break time, anyway," Kebert coaxed.

"It isn't a game for kids," Dusty warned. "Especially those kind."

"Hold on there, Morton, with that talk." Carl's eyes narrowed with warning. He sat back and thought for a moment and then smiled. "I tell you what, Morton. Why don't you and Barry play one hand? And we'll up the stakes. How about a five dollar ante? Fifty cent limit and three bumps. You can even call the game," Carl challenged.

"I'm not playin' with any feeble-minded kid. It wouldn't be fair to him," Dusty argued.

Carl looked at Dusty and grinned. "No, no, go ahead. I'll back my boy."

"You won't give him any coaching, right? You do and the game's forfeited." Dusty turned to the rest of the men. "You heard him say it."

"I'm not going to give Barry any help. It's up to him totally," Carl assured him.

Dusty shrugged. "I feel like a real chump takin' money from a feeble-minded kid. But, then again, it's really his old man I'm rimmin', so what the hay?" Dusty said, with a grin.

Barry took Carl's seat. He placed his short, chubby arms on the table and looked at Dusty and grimaced. He tried to focus his eyes, but the beer and cigars made it difficult.

"Okay, everybody, stand back." Dusty pulled his visor low and snapped the rubber bands on his upper shirt sleeves. "Here's where we separate the men from the boys. Here's the game we're playin', kid." He paused and smoothed his thin mustache. "Seven card stud, one-eyed jacks and low card in the hole wild, natural pair of sevens take all, three bump fifty cent limit, ante five bucks." Dusty turned to the men and winked.

Barry hiccuped and swayed in his chair for a moment and then anted the five dollars Carl had given him.

Dusty dealt two cards down and one up.

"The kid gets a nine of hearts and old Dusty gets a one-eyed Jack." Dusty looked at Barry. "Remember, kid, that one's wild so with that you know I've got three of a kind at least with that low wild card in the hole."

Barry looked up at Dusty and grimaced.

"Jeez, I wish he wouldn't do that," Dusty complained. "It makes me nervous. It's like he tasted somethin' sour or some-thin'."

Barry looked at him, smiled, and hiccuped.

"Okay, I'll be easy on you," Dusty said. "No one's goin' to accuse old Dusty of takin' advantage of a kid."

"Barry threw in a chip and then tossed in a another chip. "I up it fifty," he said.

Dusty chortled with glee. "That kid is really off. You'd better watch him, Wadonelli, or he'll break you."

Dusty threw in a chip. "Just call." He dealt two more cards, one to each of them. "Okay ... to the kid goes a five of clubs and to the old pro goes an ace." He turned and gave everybody a toothy grin. "That makes me at least three aces, kid. Aren't you even goin' to look at your two down cards?"

Barry grimaced and stuck out his tongue. Clumsily, he looked at the two down cards as instructed.

"Jeez, there he goes again. Okay, I bet fifty cents," Dusty said.

Barry yawned. "I bet fifty more." He shoved in chips until everyone yelled for him to stop.

Dusty preened his mustache. "The kid doesn't know anything

102

about cards." He shook his head and chuckled. "Okay, I'll see your fifty and bump you fifty more."

Barry studied his chips and pushed them in. "I up you fifty more."

"Call," Dusty said in an irritated tone. "Don't you know he's goin' to get cleaned out. Must be thirteen, fourteen bucks in there right now." Dusty threw Barry a seven of diamonds and another ace to himself. "Jeez! What luck! I wish all of you jakes were in this. I'd clean up." He looked at Barry. "You know, kid, that I have at least four aces, maybe more."

Barry grimaced and looked confused.

"Bet fifty."

"Up fifty."

"Bump you fifty."

"Bump you fifty."

"Call," Dusty said, adjusting his visor. "Last card up, kid. We're nearing the grand finale as they say. Here's your nine of spades. That makes you at least three nines. Don't look good next to my four aces or more does it? This time I get a two of clubs. Kinda hurts my five aces unless that low card in the hole happens to be a two also." Dusty leaned forward fingering his mustache. "Suppose so, kid?" He grinned and looked about, but received no encouragement.

Carl shuffled his feet about realizing he needed to go to the bathroom but was afraid to leave. He wished he hadn't pushed this quite so far.

"Okay," Dusty said, pulling his visor even lower and snapping the rubber bands on his sleeves. "This is it. This card is down and dirty."

Barry picked up his card. Dusty chuckled to himself as he looked at another ace. The tip of his tongue played with his mustache.

Barry stared down at his cards and hiccuped.

Dusty looked back and forth and for the first time had a concerned expression on his face. He studied Barry's cards. "I'll make it easy on you, kid. Bet just a quarter this time."

Barry looked at Dusty's cards and grimaced. The tension started to mount in the room.

"Jeez! There must be close to twenty, twenty-five bucks in that pot and half of it is mine."

Barry pushed in his chips with his palm. "Up fifty."

"Ah, kid, come on." Dusty turned to Carl. "Check the kid's cards. I don't want to take any more of your hard earned money."

Carl shook his head and took a deep breath. "No, that isn't the deal. Barry started on his own and he'll finish on his own one way or the other."

"Go ahead and fold for him. No use losin' any more." Dusty had a pained look on his face.

There was a long pause and no one said anything.

Dusty hunched his shoulders and tossed in fifty cents. "Okay, if that's the way you want it. Bump you fifty."

Barry pushed in more chips without hesitation. "Up fifty more."

Dusty frowned and moved his visor up on his head. He drew a handkerchief out of his back pocket and wiped his beaded forehead. "Let me see here. What you got?" Dusty's steely eyes studied Barry's cards. His eye paused on the seven. "I said sevens take all, didn't I? Now you understand they have to be naturals. The wild card doesn't work to pair 'em up," he reminded.

Barry looked at his cards and hiccuped.

"Be just like a kid to have a seven in the hole. Why in the hell did I say that, anyway?" Dusty growled beneath his breath.

Everyone moved to the edge of his seat. Carl looked at Barry but got no indication one way or the other.

"Does the kid know his numbers, Wadonelli?" Dusty asked worriedly.

Carl shrugged. "I think he knows one through ten."

Another long pause prevailed. The smoke was as thick as fog in the room.

Dusty looked at Barry's cards again and then at his expressionless face. Finally, he slammed his cards down on the table.

"Fold! I 'm not losin' any more money. The ninny had that pair of sevens all along." Dusty winced and snapped the rubber bands on his sleeves. "Jeez, the money I threw into that pot! Just plain blind luck."

Barry grinned as he raked in the huge pile of chips and cash. Carl started to throw Barry's cards in the discard pile only to have Dusty's fist come crashing down on his hand. "I paid a lot. I want to see those cards. By damn, I deserve it."

"He doesn't have to show them to you, Morton. You know the rules," reminded Leonard.

"Horse manure! I don't care. I got out with five aces. I want to see his hand!" Dusty shouted.

"You want to show your cards to Dusty, Barry?" Carl asked.

Barry nodded and grinned.

Dusty grabbed the down cards and turned them over. He searched through the cards with desperation. "All you got here is three nines! Where's that seven in the hole?"

Barry grimaced and stuck out his tongue. "I bluff."

Ollie's falsetto voice caught and then shrieked with laughter. He clutched Kebert whose face was already flushed to the point of exploding. Lennie and Charlie pounded each other on the back wheezing with laughter. Carl doubled up with uncontained hilarity. Dusty sat there stunned, a constipated look on his face.

Barry looked around at everyone, bewildered with all the ruckus.

Dusty pushed back his chair, threw money on the table to cover his chips, paused with white-hot hatred in his eyes, and then bolted out the door.

Laughter continued unabated for five more minutes. Everyone sank to the floor in wild seizures of mirth. Meanwhile, Barry polished off everyone's beer.

At last, Ollie wiped the tears from his eyes. "That was a classic." He patted Barry on the back. "Barry's the hero tonight!"

Kebert tried to compose himself and choked. "That was a once-in-a-lifetime deal."

Everyone gathered around Barry congratulating him on his

victory. Carl planted a kiss on his bald head.

"He deserves something," Lennie announced. "The hero always gets his reward. What would you like most right now, Barry? Just name it."

Barry's eyes tried to focus. He looked up at the blurred, smiling faces. "Beer," he said.

Joan tiptoed lightly into the dark house. She saw the remnants of the party throughout. A haze of smoke still lingered in the room. Bottles were strewn about. Crushed pretzels and smashed cheese was on the kitchen tile. Poker chips were scattered about. Pete lay in a corner sound asleep.

She stepped easily into the bedroom vowing to clean up the mess in the morning. The sound of snoring permeated the room. Barry lay tucked beneath Carl's heavy arm. She crept over and pecked Carl on the cheek. He didn't budge. She then moved to the other side of the bed and bent down to kiss Barry. As she leaned close to his cheek, he hiccuped and the strong, pungent smell of sour beer burned her nostrils. He smiled in his sleep and mumbled contentedly.

Joan lunged back and grabbed her mouth. "My god, he's drunk!"

Chapter 11

Carl held Barry's hand as they walked toward the dugout of the Trojans. Charley Nelson, hitting pop flies to the infield, noticed Carl and Barry entering the field. Barry wore a red baseball cap and white jersey, the colors of the Trojans.

Charley came loping up to them. "Hey, man, glad you could make it." He looked down at Barry. "Hello, there, poker face," he said. Playfully, he punched Barry in the stomach. "Have you seen Morton since Wednesday night, Carl? I'll bet his face is still red from embarrassment. It was about time someone put that windbag in his place." Charley started to chuckle. "I laughed all the way home. I even woke up Marge when I got home and told her. She thought it was hysterical. He was way overdue for somethin' like that."

Carl rubbed Barry's back with affection. "Ah, it wasn't anything much. The kid just knows his poker, that's all."

Barry grimaced and stuck out his tongue.

"I got raked over the coals the morning after," Carl added. "Joan said that Barry was drunk." He looked down at Barry, puzzled. "I tell you; I never saw him drink a thing. Maybe a sip or two that I gave him before you guys came, but certainly not enough to get him drunk."

Barry grinned and concentrated on the players batting practice.

"Has the kid ever played ball before, Carl?" Charley asked.

Carl frowned. "Gee, I don't know. Let me ask him." He turned Barry toward him with a hand on his shoulder. "Barry, have you ever played any ball before?"

Barry looked up at Carl. "I like baseball. I play sometimes."

Carl slapped him on the back. "The kid can do anything, Charley. I never saw such a kid. He can fish, play poker, even save a kid's life." He pointed. "My son, here, can do anything." He playfully pulled the bill of Barry's cap down over his eyes.

Charley grinned. "I believe you're right." He looked around. "Here, let me get my kid over here so he can meet Barry."

Charley called out to a handsome, dark-haired boy playing shortstop. The boy jogged toward his dad yelling instructions to the rest of the team.

"Brian, this boy is Carl Wadonelli's adopted kid, Barry. He came out to lend the team a hand."

Brian looked Barry up and down and then looked at his dad, puzzled.

Charley cleared his throat after a long, uncomfortable pause. "Brian, why don't you line Barry up with the team and let him have some batting practice?"

Brian started to protest but the stern, silent warning from his father deterred him. He nodded for Barry to follow him.

Barry stood for a moment, awaiting his brain to signal the correct response. Carl guided him toward the back of the line waiting to bat. He patted him on the shoulder.

"Show 'em what you can do, son," he said. "I'll be right over there with Charley. Your mom is in the stands, rooting for you." Carl pointed to Joan sitting under a wide-brimmed straw hat.

Barry looked up, waved, and shouted, "Hi, Mama Wadi! Hi! Mama Wadi!"

Joan looked over her sun glasses and waved back enthusiastically.

The entire Trojan team turned and stared in disbelief at this strange boy lined up to bat with their team. Charley's son ran to his dad with an angry look on his face. Carl saw that an animated discussion was in progress between father and son. At last, Charley gave Brian a push back to the line of ball players. Brian walked back with his shoulders slumped and a scowl on his face.

Carl pulled at the bill of his cap nervously as Barry took his position at the plate. Everyone in the stands sat forward caught up in this turn of events. A cynical smirk came to Brian's face as Barry clumsily laid the bat on his shoulder and faced the pitcher. Charley ran out to assist Barry. Carl crossed his fingers as Barry listened intently as Charley explained the appropriate way to grip the bat and take a stance.

The first ball flew by him at the belt. Barry turned and grimaced at the catcher. The second pitch streaked by him and he chopped at the air after the thud was heard in the catcher's mit. Sniggers and chortles were heard from the stands and from the opposing team. Brian turned his head and glared at his dad. Carl bit into his lower lip. He noticed again Barry's hunched shoulders, hairless body, slanted eyes, pugged nose, and strange mannerisms. He noticed the difference in Barry compared to the handsome, bright, athletic players on the team. He noticed the stark difference to Ricky. Glancing up in the stands, Carl caught the anguish on Joan's face.

Carl pulled his cap lower and crouched to view Barry's stance. This was his son, for better or for worse, he told himself. He remembered Mrs. Bertrand's words: "There will be frustration and disappointment, but if you expect a lot you will be rewarded with a lot." He straightened his shoulders and clapped his hands. "Let's go, Barry. Show 'em, son. Hit that potato out of the park!"

Joan looked at Carl from the stands and a wave of pride produced goose pimples on her bare arms. She pulled her dark glasses from her eyes and shouted to Barry. "Come on, Barry, hit that potato out of the park!"

A smile came to Carl's face. He looked up at Joan and threw her a kiss.

Barry grimaced and concentrated on the pitcher's windup. The ball shot at him. He poised himself and took an awkward upward swing at the ball. Barry caught a small part of the ball and it rose skyward to shallow left field where the fielder made an easy play. Carl jumped with joy as Joan screeched with delight. Barry ran, hunched, to first base his tongue hanging out of the corner of his mouth. He stood there with a wide grin on his face. Several of the players tried to persuade him that he was out but Barry remained on first clapping his hands and grinning. Finally, Carl walked up to him and put his arm around his shoulders. Barry looked up from beneath the shaded bill of his cap and grimaced.

"Son," Carl said, "you're out. They caught the ball."

Barry looked up, confused.

"When you hit the ball and they catch it, you're out. If they would've missed it, you would be safe." Carl took Barry's chin and pulled it to him so they faced each other eye to eye. "Do you understand?"

A sad expression came to Barry's face. It was the first time Carl had seen him look sad since the day they returned him to St. Vincents. Barry hunched his shoulders and walked back to the dugout with Carl.

Charley called the team in for a final pep talk and Barry crowded in with them.

Carl sat on the bench through eight innings, cheering, helping with equipment problems, coaching first, rubbing sore muscles, and applying first aid when needed. Barry followed him like a shadow. Sweat coursed off of his brow and into his eyes. Even when the score was unbalanced in favor of the Trojans, Barry tensed over every pitch. He ran up to players who came home and patted them on their back. For those who struck out, Barry offered consolation and "better luck next time". Carl and Barry got so involved in the game and the team that they forgot about Barry playing.

At the bottom of the eighth inning with the score of the Trojans 18 and the Bombers 3, Barry's name was called by Charley Nelson. Barry sat there until he was prodded by Carl's elbow. Then he sprang to his feet and walked hunched to the plate. The loud speaker announced a line-up change. "Wadonelli hitting for Nelson."

Joan cheered uncontrollably. Carl's chest inflated with pride.

His eyes acquired a coating of moisture. Everyone on the team screamed encouragement.

Barry's thick tongue hung out of the corner of his mouth as he concentrated on the pitch. The first pitch caught the outside corner for a strike. Barry chopped at it after the ball was already tucked in the catcher's glove. Barry tightened his grip. The second pitch was a fast ball, strike. Barry's hazy brain failed to realize it until the ball was back in the pitcher's glove. Carl clenched his fists with tension. Joan covered her eyes in the stands. She peeked shyly through her spread fingers.

The third pitch was too low, a ball. Barry beamed with pride as Carl shouted praise for good judgment. He clutched the bat and grimaced. The pitcher wound up for the fourth pitch and let the ball fly. It curved inward directly at Barry. His slow reaction did not give him enough time to get out of the way and the ball caught him on the shin. Barry grabbed his leg and buckled to the dirt. The coach, Carl, and the team gathered around him. Joan held her head in her hands and moaned.

Barry looked up at the faces staring down at him. He grinned. "I get to walk," he announced proudly.

The coach and the team clapped him on the back and sent him hobbling to first base.

The inning ended before Barry got to second base but Carl felt good. He realized that Barry was a real trooper. Not a tear was shed when the ball slammed into him. Yessir ... a real trooper, he thought. Carl stared down at his feet as another realization came into focus. Barry was mentally handicapped and had limited capabilities. He would never be a good ball player. He would never hit the ball a country mile in the Cookie league or any other league like Ricky. Good ball playing took quick thinking and lightning reflexes. Barry could not coax his mind to assist him at times. Carl shrugged with resolve. For some reason, it didn't matter to him. At least he had been part of the team today.

Joan gathered her thermos of cold tea and stadium chair and ran to Carl and Barry just leaving the dugout. She wiped Barry's flushed, sweaty face with her handkerchief. Instructing him to raise his pants leg, she examined the bruised shin.

Carl reprimanded her for fawning over him. "Joan, leave the boy alone. He isn't a baby."

"He isn't an adult, either. He's just a boy and a mother is concerned over her son's injuries." She carefully felt the leg.

"I got on base, Mama Wadi," Barry said, smiling.

Joan frowned. "I know and I'm proud of you. But, you almost got killed doing it. I thought baseball was a safe game."

Charley lumbered up and placed his hand on Carl's shoulder. "How's the kid," he asked. "He took a real blow on that leg. Not a whimper from him. That kid's got guts."

Carl turned and looked at Charley, noticing a nervous twitch beneath his left eye. They had been friends for years and Carl knew Charley was about to tell him something that he didn't want to.

"What's wrong, Charley," he asked.

Charley winced and placed his hand on Carl's shoulder once again.

Carl shrugged Charley's hand away. "Just come out with it. We've known each other too many years to beat around the bush."

Charley picked at a mole on his chin nervously. "Well, Carl, you know me. I'm always for the underdog. Remember when I was a kid I always helped Seymore Perkins, that little sissy, fight the bullies. I was always for the guy who couldn't quite do it. I was always for the guy everyone gave a hard time. I was always for the ..."

"Handicapped?" Carl interjected.

Charley hung his head and kicked at the dirt with the toe of his shoe.

Carl placed his hand on Charley's shoulder this time. "Don't be down. I know what you're going to say. You're trying to tell me Barry isn't good enough to play on the team."

"Maybe he could help as manager or bat boy or somethin'," Charley offered.

"You don't have to throw Barry a bone, Charley. He and I both know that he can't ever come up to normal kids in every way. In fact, it took today to bring that home to me." Carl smiled to himself and then looked at Joan. "You see, Charley, that's okay. Joan and I know Barry's mentally handicapped. He knows he's mentally handicapped. Nobody's kidding anybody." He looked away for a moment. "Joan and I love Barry, not because he's the smartest kid or the best ball player or even best at anything. We love him because of who he is."

Joan reached out and squeezed Carl's arm.

"Barry's the best thing that could have happened to us. After Rick died, we were dead also. He's done more for us than we could ever do for him. So, don't feel bad. You gave him a chance. He didn't measure up, that's all." He playfully pulled Barry's cap bill down over his eyes. "But, he's mighty special in a whole lot of other ways. He's our kid and we're behind him all of the way."

Charley opened his mouth to speak, but no words came out.

Carl playfully tipped back Barry's cap and he looked up and smiled. He seemed confused with all of the serious conversation.

Carl encircled his shoulders with one arm and Joan's shoulders with the other and together they walked across the field to their truck.

Charley pulled off his cap and scratched his head with bewilderment.

Chapter 12

Joan sang a little song she learned as a child. It occurred to her that she had not thought about it in thirty years. It had a simple melody, but it conjured up pleasant memories from her past.

As she wiped the kitchen table, she craned her neck to watch Barry vacuum the living room carpet. His tongue stuck out of his mouth as it always did when he was deep in concentration.

The hum of the vacuum cleaner was a comforting, domestic sound. She agreed that Barry had become a good helper. She watched as he carefully maneuvered the vacuum around a slumbering, immobile Pete who refused to move even when Barry nudged him. Joan giggled under her breath as she watched Barry's puzzlement on how to handle the situation. He nudged Pete under his chin and then under his drooping posterior with no results. Pete lay there steadfast, refusing to budge, pretending he was in the depths of sleep. Finally, Barry placed the vacuum on his head and it instantly inhaled his long, flaccid ears. Pete's eyes popped open in terror as he felt his ears being sucked into the vacuum nozzle. He yipped in fright and bolted across the room to the safety and seclusion of the closet. Barry continued his household chores without a bit of amusement on his face.

Joan felt exhilarated because on Monday she was to attend a parent's night at Barry's school. She could not help but feel proud of him. He would not divulge the title of the play they were putting on nor the plot even after an hour of questioning. Carl was going with her. He was going to rush his chores that evening so they would have plenty of time to get ready.

Joan was proud of Carl; he was a changed man since Barry had entered their lives. When Ricky had died, he had submerged himself in the farm so he would not have to think about his sadness. But now, the farm did not monopolize all of his time, thoughts, and energy. He gave time to her and to Barry.

Joan was also aware that she had changed. She felt a closeness to Carl these days. She felt that after Ricky died there was a coldness in their relationship. It seemed that their sorrow and despair took everything they had and left them with no will, no energy for their relationship. She thought Carl was a great father. Perhaps, he was even a better father with Barry than he was with Ricky. Barry needed more care and instruction, whereas, Ricky was more self-sufficient.

Joan looked forward now to each day because it held so much fun and promise. Mrs. Bertrand had been perfectly right, she thought. Having Barry around was like having perpetual sunshine. A hug, a smile, a giggle from him always lifted her spirits.

She loved to teach him, even though simple tasks sometimes had to be repeated dozens of times before he mastered them. Joan would watch him as he tried so hard to print his name, count money, dial the telephone, make his bed, or tie his shoes. These were just a few of the basics of everyday living that nearly everyone took for granted. But, for Barry, these were monumental tasks that took hours of tedious struggling before victory was achieved. After each of these tasks were fought for and won, Joan would beam with pride for Barry and for herself. She was amazed at her resilience and patience. Learning had come so easily for Ricky. She felt like Barry, Carl, and she were a team ... and a pretty good one at that.

After these few months, Joan couldn't imagine not having Barry. It was as though he had been with them for years. Perhaps, it was because now life held more importance and significance. There was more to it than just eating, sleeping, working ... existing. It was true. Barry was giving them far more than they were giving him.

Barry switched off the vacuum cleaner and turned to Joan, unaware that she had been watching him for the past ten minutes.

"Mama Wadi, I done. Does it look good?" he asked in his graveled voice. He pointed to the rug he had just cleaned.

Joan went in and examined the carpet. She noticed dog hair and lint in one corner of the room that he missed. She looked at his happy, proud face and wanted to heap praise on him. She remembered what Mrs. Bertrand had said about expecting little and getting little in return.

"Sweetheart, it's a fine job except for that corner over there." She pointed. "You missed some lint and some of Pete's hair. Why don't you get that and then it will look fine."

With a nod, he turned the vacuum on once again and started going over the place she pointed to.

After the vacuuming, it was time for Barry to help with the breakfast dishes. She watched as he dried each plate with meticulous care. She noticed how mechanical his movements were. An ant traveled across the kitchen counter and his interest was absorbed in its slow trek.

"Barry, you're getting behind," she warned. "Pay attention so we can get the dishes finished. I have to check and see how you made your bed."

Barry brought his attention back to the plate in his hand. But, out of the corner of his eye, he continued watching the ant until it disappeared behind the sink.

He paused and looked up at the cabinet trying to recall where to put the saucer he had finished drying. Joan started to tell him the location, but hesitated when she remembered his teacher's instructions about letting him do as much as possible on his own. His squinted eyes looked up at the cupboard doors trying to recall where to put the saucer. Finally, a smile came to his face as he pointed to the correct door. Joan kissed his head affectionately. Barry pulled a kitchen chair over and started to climb on it to reach the shelf. Joan frowned. He shoved the chair back in place and got the stool. Joan then smiled and nodded her approval.

Sometimes, Joan felt like the wicked witch. How much easier it would be to dress, feed, and bathe him. How much less work and strain it would be to allow him to sit in front of the TV while she did the housework and all of the chores. But, Barry was twelve years old, an adolescent, and he must be trained to one day face a sheltered workshop situation where he could live and earn a living. They told her being firm was being kind because you were preparing him for later life and he must be ready. He wasn't going to be the cute, roly-poly child forever. He must be prepared to be as self-sufficient as possible. All of the self help skills must be attained. They must tap every potential of his hazy brain to get as many correct responses as possible.

Barry followed Joan into his bedroom. She turned to him with a scowl on her face. "Look at that mess! You have the blankets dragging on the floor on one side and nothing at all on the other side. Look at the lumps in the bed and your pillowcase is half off the pillow! This is the worst your bed has looked in weeks."

Barry hung his head in shame. Joan bit the inside of her lip and doubled her fists in frustration. She wanted to rush over to him and comfort him and tell him it didn't matter. But, she knew that she must not.

"For this mess, Barry, you can not watch Bozo the Clown on TV today."

Barry glanced up as a sullen expression came to his face. Tears formed in his eyes. He stomped his feet and shouted: "I hate Mama Wadi! I hate Mama Wadi! I go back to Sister. She nicer ... she nicer!" He ran to his bed and began pulling off the blankets and flinging them to the floor.

Joan's temper, which had been submerged for a long time, rocketed to the surface. She grabbed his arm and held him still while she deposited several sound whacks on his chubby buttocks. Barry let out a howl as though he were being killed.

"You can stay in your room until you learn to behave and until you can make your bed right!" Joan closed the door behind her, trembling with rage intermingled with guilt. This was the biggest upset she had had so far with him. She heard him sobbing through the door and it was all she could do to keep herself from rushing to him and consoling him. Pete lumbered up to the door and sniffed at it and started to whine sensing his good friend was in trouble.

Joan tried to busy herself with other household tasks, but kept eyeing Barry's room. It had suddenly gotten silent and she started to worry. She sat on the divan and folded clothes at a furious pace. Her ear was attuned to any sound in Barry's room. Still there was nothing but silence. Pete scratched on Barry's door but the door remained closed. Joan continued folding clothes all the while staring at the closed door. At last, she could contain herself no longer. She started toward Barry's room. As she reached for the knob, the door swung open. Barry rushed out and grabbed her around the waist and gave her a vigorous hug. Joan gasped in surprise.

"I sorry, Mama Wadi. I sorry," Barry apologized. "I love Mama Wadi. I not hate her."

Joan caressed him and kissed him on the cheek.

He looked up and broke into a grin. "Mama Wadi, come see my bed." He tugged at her hand and Joan followed him into his room. The bed was made almost perfectly with just one small lump in the middle. Toto's head rested on the pillow at the head of the bed.

Joan held him to her and hugged him with pride. Another small victory had been achieved.

Carl bounded through the kitchen door wiping his forehead with a bandanna he pulled from the back pocket of his jeans.

Joan looked up from her ironing.

"Just ran in to get Barry and me something cold to drink. It's as hot as heck out there," he said, wiping his neck and then dipping the cloth down his open shirt.

"Where are you working today?" she asked, running the iron

deftly around a shirt collar.

"Barry and I are up in the south pasture checking on the cattle up there." Pulling the refrigerator door open, he took out two bottles of pop.

"There's some cookies in the cabinet. Take the box; Barry loves Oreos," Joan instructed.

"Good idea." Carl pulled the cabinet door open and took out the box of cookies. He shook his head, smiling to himself. "That kid is something. I let him drive the John Deere there and back like Rick used to do."

Joan looked up. "What do you mean, drive it?"

Carl pried the cap off the bottle of Coke and tipped it to his lips. "Oh, you know. I shifted the gears and everything and sat next to him. What he did was steer, actually, but he had a ball."

Joan smiled. "I'll bet he did. He loves being outside working with you."

Carl nodded. "You know, I think next spring he might be able to do a little plowing and planting if I work with him a lot until then."

Joan's brow wrinkled. "Be careful, hon. Remember, he's not Ricky. It'll take him a lot more time and training than Ricky."

He nodded. "Oh, sure. I know that. I'll take it one step at a time. I wouldn't think of letting him drive the tractor by himself for a long time yet. I'll be right by his side until I know he's good and ready."

"Sometimes, I think we forget that mentally he's only about four years old. We need to remind ourselves of that every once in awhile so we don't expect too much out of him," Joan said, placing the shirt on a metal hanger.

Carl pushed the bill of his cap back with a thumb. "You're right, there. It's just that he's so darned eager. All the way up there and back he kept asking to do it by himself. He can be a very persuasive kid."

Joan threw her head back, laughing. "I know. I find myself giving in to him all of the time."

"It was something, Joan. Pete followed us up there and all the

120

way back. And I'm talking about several miles. I can't believe the energy that old dog has these days."

"Are they out in the yard playing?" Joan asked.

"Yeah. I left the tractor running while I ran in here to get something to drink. I want to put it back in the shed and then go burn some brush."

"But, where's Barry and Pete?" she asked, setting down the iron.

"I told you. I left them outside while I ran in here."

"But where, Carl?" Joan asked, with a tinge of concern in her voice.

"Just look out the window. You'll see them," Carl said, pointing to the kitchen window. "They're probably wrestling around in the yard like they always do."

Joan walked to the window and looked out. She rotated her head one way and then another to look in both directions. "I don't see them, Carl."

"You must be blind. They're right out there in front." Carl went to the window and looked out. He stretched his neck to look in all directions.

"Do you see them?" Joan asked.

"No." Suddenly, he stiffened, turned, and bolted out of the kitchen door without any explanation.

"What? What's the matter?" Joan shouted.

Carl turned and called back over his shoulder. "I don't see them and I don't see the tractor either!"

Joan pulled the plug on the iron and raced behind him. "My god, where are they?"

Carl and Joan ran to the gate. They gasped as their eyes widened with disbelief. In the distance they saw Barry driving the tractor, weaving one way and then another. Pete was running alongside barking frantically.

"My god!" Carl yelled. "He got the tractor in gear somehow!"

Joan watched in dread, her heart pounding in her chest. "Do something, Carl! He doesn't know a thing about driving. He'll be killed!"

Carl darted forward racing after the tractor. He ran, shouting for him to stop and then remembered Barry knew nothing about stopping the machine.

"Barry! Barry! Slow down, son!" he shouted.

Carl finally moved even with Barry running alongside the tractor. Looking up, he saw Barry's wide, excited grin.

Barry lifted his cap from his head, waved it in the air, and shouted. "Yahoo! Yahoo! Look, Daddy Wadi! I'm driving!"

Pete ran with Carl, continuing his nonstop barking. At times, Carl's feet got tangled up with him.

Joan ran toward them too frightened to make a sound. She pressed her fingers to her lips and prayed.

Barry continued shouting and waving his cap in the air. The speed he was traveling was too fast to enable Carl to jump on the vehicle and take control.

Carl felt himself tire as sweat coursed down his face. "Turn the wheel, Barry! Turn the wheel! Turn the tractor around, son!" he shouted.

"I try, Daddy Wadi." Barry plopped his cap back on his head and cranked the steering wheel sharply to the right. His face reddened with the effort.

The tractor turned abruptly in a circle and reversed its course.

Carl gulped, finding the tractor now behind him instead of in front of him as before. The huge vehicle loomed down upon him.

"Oh, god, no," he moaned, lifting his feet as high and as fast as he could, racing to get away.

Joan closed her eyes. The tractor was only a short distance behind Carl's flying feet. Pete barked out of control and Barry shouted and waved his cap with excitement. It was obvious that he was having the time of his life.

Carl headed for the outbuildings, the tractor still nudging his heels. He lost his cap a long time ago and his hair flew in the wind. His face was beet-red and he heaved with deep, explosive breaths.

Suddenly, Carl stumbled and fell on his face. The Prayer of

Contrition flashed through his mind as he plummeted to the hard ground.

The tractor continued bearing down upon him. With surprising presence of mind, Carl rolled to one side. Looking up, the huge wheels flashed past him heading straight toward the chicken coop.

Carl sat up. His voice caught in his throat, watching helplessly, as the tractor charged into the chicken coop. The sound of the impact was deafening.

Chickens squawked and flew from all directions out of the big, gaping hole in the wall. Pete raced about frantically barking in deep, stuccato tones.

A chill raced through Joan. Her legs started to shake. She removed her hands from her eyes and looked at the incredible scene before her. Carl sat on the ground staring at the chicken coop in disbelief. Pete practically turned himself inside out with excitement. Chickens flew from every direction in a frenzy. Feathers floated in the air.

The hood and front wheels of the tractor set embedded in the chicken coop wall. There were splintered boards laying about everywhere.

Barry screamed at the top of his lungs and waved his cap in the air.

"Yahoo! Yahoo! I drive the tractor, Daddy Wadi!" he yelled.

Joan's legs buckled beneath her and she limply folded to the ground holding her head in her hands.

Chapter 13

Carl's sharp aftershave saturated the air of the classroom. Joan thought he looked very handsome tonight. His black curly hair was oiled and combed. He had on his Sunday suit and his polka dot tie. She could almost see her face in the shine of his shoes which he had brushed diligently for half an hour.

Carl shifted in his chair. He ran a finger around his stiff collar trying to pull it away from his neck. The only time he put on a suit and tie was for church. He, Joan, and Barry never missed mass on Sundays. Barry seemed to enjoy it and always sang out joyously.

There was an audible mumbling of anticipation by the assembled parents. Joan looked around to the row behind her and looked straight into the eyes of Nelda Bertrand. They let out simultaneous squeals of recognition. Mrs. Bertrand hurried toward her with a pleased smile.

"I knew it, I just knew it. You kept him, didn't you?" Mrs. Bertrand asked.

Carl nodded and laughed. "We could no more get rid of that kid than anything."

"Is Amy in Barry's class, Mrs. Bertrand?" Joan asked.

"No." Mrs. Bertrand shook her head. "She goes to Green Oaks in Stockton but Mrs. Pinkerton invited the parents of Green Oaks children to come over tonight. I try to attend as many things for mentally handicapped kids as I can. We belong to the ARC ... Association for Retarded Citizens which is a marvelous organization for retarded people and parents. It gives everyone a common bond and you can keep up on things for the mentally handicapped. I think you folks would really like it. " Mrs. Bertrand paused for a moment. "And then later on next summer there will be the Special Olympics. That is a beautiful sight."

"Special Olympics?" asked Carl. "What's that?"

"Well, it's an organization sponsored by the Kennedy Foundation," Mrs. Bertrand explained. "It is international in scope and open to all mentally handicapped people. They have events ranging from wheelchair races, to swimming, to relays, for the special athletes. There are regional meets and then huge state meets with thousands of people attending. And there are even international meets." Mrs. Bertrand smiled. "Oh, it's just spectacular at the state meets. They have a lighted torch held by a mentally handicapped person who runs up the stadium steps and lights the flame opening the games, just like the regular Olympics. And then hundreds of retarded people with ages ranging from small children to the elderly take part in all kinds of track and field events. It gives each one of them a wonderful feeling of worthiness and value. You see people there much more handicapped than Barry and Amy and it makes one feel very fortunate. I've seem children who had to be guided around the track by someone, but they finish and are cheered by the crowd and they smile proudly. They present them with ribbons and medals. I always get goose bumps when they stand and receive their bronze, silver, and gold medals. It's their time to be proud of themselves."

Joan looked at this lady who seemed so at peace with herself. "I think Carl and I would like Barry to get involved in something like that. It sounds wonderful."

"Oh, it is," Mrs. Bertrand said. "There will be publicity about it during the year at school. They will send home forms for you folks to fill out. I know Barry would like it."

"Where's Amy tonight?" Carl inquired.

"She's at home with a bad chest cold. My husband stayed with her. She wanted to come. And I know when I tell her that Barry was here, she will really be upset. She's told everybody how he pulled her out of the lake and saved her life." Mrs. Bertrand's face grew solemn. "You know, if it weren't for Barry, we might have lost Amy."

Joan smiled proudly. "He is quite a kid; I'll tell you that. It's like you said a couple of months ago: he's sunshine insurance."

Mrs. Bertrand squeezed Joan's hand. I'm so glad you both feel that way. I knew if you gave him a chance you'd find that out."

A sudden bank of tears came to Mrs. Bertrand's eyes. "I'm sort of jittery tonight. Every time Amy gets sick, I go off the deep end. She's very frail even though she looks healthy. She's had pneumonia three times and has come close to death each time. I guess you just have to have faith." She tried to smile.

Mrs. Pinkerton walked out in front of the parents and the room became quiet. "Welcome all of the parents of our children and welcome also to the parents and children of Green Oaks. We are happy you could attend. The children have been preparing these skits for weeks and were sworn to secrecy about the theme." She looked around. "Just out of curiosity, will you raise your hand if the theme of our program was revealed to you by your child?"

Everyone turned and looked around, but no hands were raised.

Mrs. Pinkerton smiled and clapped her hands. "I knew I could trust them. Well, I'll let you in on it now. We are going to act out various nursery rhymes. I will narrate the nursery rhymes and the children will act out the various roles." Mrs. Pinkerton paused and focused her eyes on Joan and Carl. "Before we start, I would like to introduce the parents of a new student in our class. May I introduce Mr. and Mrs. Carl Wadonelli, parents of Barry, who by the way, will be Humpty Dumpty in our first nursery rhyme? Would you please stand?" She nodded toward Joan and Carl.

They stood and were received by warm applause. Mrs. Bertrand applauded the loudest and with the most enthusiasm. Joan felt a large obstruction block her throat as tears welled in her eyes. She reached down and clasped Carl's hand as they sat down.

The lights dimmed and the first skit started. The spot light focused on Barry wearing a huge cardboard eggshell on his head sitting on a wooden box representing a brick wall. He squinted his eyes as he looked into the bright light and grimaced. Goose bumps of pride appeared on Joan's arms.

Mrs. Pinkerton started the narration. "Humpty Dumpty sat on a wall. Humpty Dumpty had a great fall ..." She nodded toward Barry and he plummeted backwards on cue, accidentally knocking off his cardboard egg shell revealing his hairless head. He now looked far more like an egg. Barry looked up from behind the wall at the audience and smiled. Everyone laughed and applauded his efforts.

Carl's chest jutted with pride. It was the same feeling he had months ago when Ricky hit a long ball into centerfield in the Cookie League.

Joan and Carl sat watching "Old King Cole," "Little Jack Horner," "Mary had a Little Lamb," and "Jack Sprat." Barry appeared in "Jack Sprat" and his partner was a little Down Syndrome girl who again looked very much like him except for her pageboy hair cut. She wore a long dress filled to capacity with pillows and rags to make her appear obese. Barry and his partner sat at a table on stage, pretending to eat their meal. The girl's plate was stacked with every kind of synthetic food while "Jack's" plate was empty except for a strip as narrow as a shoestring representing lean meat.

Everyone applauded the efforts of the children as the lights snapped on and they lined up together to take a bow.

Joan and Carl directed their attention to Barry as his name was announced and he bowed low. Joan noticed how happy and unpretentious these children were. Mrs. Bertrand was perfectly right about them being God's Chosen Children.

The ten children went to a backroom to change out of their costumes and Mrs. Pinkerton came out to talk to the parents. "I think you all have so much to be proud of tonight. The children are doing a fine job this year so far. Much of the credit goes to you parents who work faithfully with them at home. Everything that we do here must be carried on and repeated over and over at home." She paused. "Be a little stern with them at times. They are not going to break like Humpty Dumpty. Make them wash those supper dishes by themselves a couple times a week, instruct them on the correct change they should receive for a purchase, make them responsible for feeding the dog, taking out the garbage, or making their bed. Don't coddle them. Love them, but don't coddle them. Don't give them something when they just point and refuse to ask for it verbally." She smiled and looked at the parents. "Most of the boys and girls here tonight are twelve and thirteen and their bodies are changing even though their minds refuse to keep pace. We are now discussing sex with them ... in simple terms of course, but not in terms of "hatched out of an egg" or "found in a cabbage patch". They are as curious as regular students. We must be truthful with them. Even though they are charming, we must keep in mind that they will someday be adults and we must, together, prepare them." Mrs. Pinkerton lowered her eyes and then looked up once again. "I want all of you to browse around the room and you will be a able to observe a few of the things we've been doing in class lately. For instance, in that corner," she pointed, "the children are practicing setting the table. Over there, they are learning how to dress themselves and tie their shoes. Over there, they have a store where they purchase items and count change. Over there, they are practicing to read and understand various public signs. And then over in that corner they are working on art projects for Christmas. It's kind of messy right now with the papier mache. Christmas is a little more than a month away, so please quickly glance at that corner because some of the projects may be eventual Christmas presents for you." Everyone laughed. "We have several field trips planned for the second half of this school year to expose the children to society and its complications and to expose society to them. I think they will do well. Just remember, expect little from them and you will be rewarded by little. Challenge them and you will both be rewarded." She paused and smiled. "Now, thank you all again for coming and feel free to browse about. Cathy and Peter are serving punch and cookies at the back table. Please let them serve you."

Barry grabbed their hands and proudly showed them his school achievements. He did, however, steer them away from the table of the Christmas projects.

Joan couldn't believe it was already time to leave. She and Carl said goodbye to Mrs. Pinkerton, Mrs. Bertrand, and the others and walked down the concrete steps from the classroom.

Barry pulled his stocking cap down over his ears as the bitter wind whipped about. He pointed to the black sky. "Look, Mama Wadi," he shouted, "it's starting to snow!"

Chapter 14

Barry sat on the floor pushing his toy cars over imaginary roads and bridges. He made rumbling noises as the cars went smoothly down straight aways and screeching sounds as they turned sharp corners. The floor was covered with toy cars, trucks, and busses. Joan was sorry that the house was so confining. She took Barry to the park as often as possible to allow him to play in the air and sunshine. He relished these times as he romped about on swings and slides. And he did get out often to help Carl and her with chores. During last month, though, the weather had turned cold and blustery and it made the out-of-doors less inviting.

A knock sounded on the front door. Joan hurried to open it, patting the back of her hair on the way. She opened the door and looked down at two boys dressed to the hilt for winter weather. Looking out, she noticed an old Ford pickup with the motor running parked in the drive. A woman nodded and waved.

"Hello," Joan said to the boys standing on the porch.

One boy immediately started a hacking, dry cough and the other one waited until he stopped before he explained their presence.

"My name is Mick Morton, Mrs. Wadonelli. This here is Donny, my brother." He pointed to the shorter boy with the cough. "We live just a mile up the road. We moved in two months ago. My dad farms the old Simmons place. My uncle is Dusty Morton. Your husband knows him, I think."

Barry watched the two boys and grimaced. Mucous ran from the short one's nose and coated his upper lip. He would snort now and then to stop its trail.

"Come in, boys, come in," Joan invited. "It's too cold to stand out there." She nodded. "Yes, my husband said some new folks moved in there. I hope you like it as well as Lawton. It's a nice town."

The two boys entered without hesitation, stomping snow off of their boots and onto the rug.

"Now, what can I do for you?" Joan asked, smiling. "Do you boys go to the same school as Barry?"

The older boy nodded. "Yeah, we see him there all of the time." He looked up from his stocking cap which was pulled low over his forehead. "We was just wonderin' if he," he pointed to Barry sitting on the floor, "would like to go into town and maybe go sledding on that hill by the park. Donny and me see him sometimes outside here and it looks like he ain't got no one to play with."

Barry grimaced and stuck out his tongue.

Joan smiled and patted the older boy's shoulder. "That's nice of you boys. I think he is about ready to climb the walls. It's been snowing for three days."

"Donny and me are going with Ma to get some groceries so we thought he could go along with us if he wanted to and then we could go over to the park and sled, maybe." He looked down at the short boy and glared.

"That sounds nice. I tell you what; I'll give you boys a half dollar a piece and you can get yourselves some candy or some-thing and when you get back, I'll have some hot chocolate ready for all of you."

"Thank you, ma'm. That sounds real good." He looked down at Barry. "Is he ready to go now?"

Joan leaned down and looked straight into Barry's eyes. "Hon, Mick and Donny want you to go to the store with them and play afterwards at the park. Would you like that?"

Barry paused. Finally, he nodded enthusiastically.

"Okay," Joan said, "go ahead and put on your coat and cap and I'll go get my purse."

Joan went to the bedroom for her purse and Barry slowly

walked to the closet and pulled his coat from the hanger.

Mick and Donny watched him as he concentrated on buttoning his coat, one button at a time with his tongue hanging out of the corner of his mouth. Mick nudged Donny with his elbow and Donny started to giggle. Mick grabbed the nape of Donny's neck and applied pressure. Donny winced and sobered at once.

"Here you are." Joan handed the older boy the coins and he stuffed them into his coat pocket. "You boys have a good time." Joan smiled. "And thank you both for inviting Barry along. It was thoughtful of you."

"That's okay," Mick said as he and Donny ushered Barry out of the door.

The door closed and Joan sighed, feeling pleased. Barry should have friends, she told herself. It wasn't good for him to always be around adults except for school. Normal children would be a good influence on him.

Joan moved the curtain back and watched the old pickup back out of the drive revving its motor and spinning its wheels.

Pete waddled up to her and started to whimper. Joan leaned over and scratched him behind his long, limp ears. "You're jealous, aren't you? You don't like Barry having any friends except you ... you old hound." She cuffed him playfully on the head.

Joan hummed happily as she picked up the vehicles strewn about the living room. She thought to herself how wonderful it was to have evidence of a child around the house again.

Joan looked at her watch worriedly. She turned the burner out from under the hot chocolate an hour ago. Barry and the boys had been gone for over two hours. She cautioned herself not to panic. Perhaps, she had misunderstood, she told herself.

Joan shrugged. She didn't know why she was getting so upset. Afterall, two hours was not all that long. And besides, she asked herself, what could happen? The older boy looked like he was at least Barry's age and fairly responsible and their mother did accompany them. Besides, Carl knew Dusty, their uncle.

Joan intentionally busied herself with cleaning the house. She straightened pictures that were not crooked, dusted lamps that were dust free, and fluffed pillows that did not need to be fluffed. She thought about going to the barn to confide in Carl but decided she did not want to worry him unnecessarily.

Joan had a roll of shelf paper out to start relining the kitchen shelves when a knock sounded on the door. Rushing to the door, she jerked it open telling herself to remain calm. She looked up into the youthful face of a police officer. He tipped his hat to her and smiled. She looked down at Barry. A mixture of relief and concern intermingled within her.

"Mrs. Wadi?" the officer inquired.

"Wadonelli," Joan answered. "What ... where did you find him? What's happened? Where are the other two boys?"

"Mrs. Wadonelli, may I come in and explain, please?" the officer asked.

"Oh, of course. I'm sorry." Joan backed away from the door allowing the officer and Barry to enter. "It's just that it's a shock to see a police officer at your front door with your child."

Pete started to wag his tail as the officer entered. Joan shooed him away and he turned and scurried to the kitchen. Barry stood there, seemingly unaffected by the circumstances.

"Please sit down, officer. Should I go get my husband?" Joan asked.

"No, I don't think that will be necessary." The officer took his hat off and sat down.

Barry pulled his cap off and sat on the floor with his legs crossed. Mucous ran from his nose and he swiped it away with his coat sleeve.

"Did he get lost? He's got an identification card in his pocket with his name and address on it."

"That's a good idea, Mrs. Wadonelli. I wish more parents would do that. It would save us a lot of time and trouble." The officer furrowed his brow and looked down at Barry. "No, Barry was caught shoplifting at Granville's Grocery on Sage."

Joan grabbed her mouth. "Oh, no! Are you sure?"

The officer nodded. "Very sure; he was caught outside the store with many unpaid items in his pockets."

Barry looked up and grimaced.

Joan glared at him. "Wait until your dad hears about this."

Barry hung his head in shame still not quite sure what he did that was wrong. But, he was sure that it was something bad.

The officer cleared his throat. "Mrs. Wadonelli, may I speak to you in private?"

Joan looked at Barry with a scowl. "Go to your bedroom right now. I will deal with you later."

Barry slowly got up and walked, hunched, toward his room. Pete came from the kitchen and followed him inside.

The officer turned to Joan. "I don't want to make a casual thing out of this, Mrs. Wadonelli, because it isn't. But, I think there are extenuating circumstances in this case."

Joan looked back at him, puzzled.

"Barry did take those things from the store but I'm almost certain he was put up to it. Those Morton brothers have a record of getting mentally handicapped kids to do their dirty work, so if they're caught there is no evidence on them. They've been trouble ever since they moved in. The whole family is ignorant and prejudiced. This has happened a couple of other times with them using mentally handicapped kids. It's a real low thing to do, but they're masters at it."

Joan was confused.

"They purposely bring retarded kids with them and tell them to take the things they want. Retarded kids, as you know, are usually gullible and trusting and will about do anything someone tells them to do. They are too trusting sometimes, for their own good." The officer nodded, subconsciously verifying his own statements. "I think this is what happened with Barry. He seems to be a kid who is normally well behaved."

Joan sighed. "We have really tried, officer. But, I know we've made mistakes. We've only had him a few months." She smiled proudly. "We're adopting him."

"That's great, Mrs. Wadonelli. He looks like a fine boy." The officer looked down for a moment in revery. "My wife and I have a little girl who is brain damaged. She's quite a handful at times, but then she can be a doll at times, too. I think the main thing we try to do is expose her to other people and situations as much as possible. Both they and she benefit from this. The days of hiding mentally handicapped people are over. In many places they are mainstreaming these children into the regular classes at school. The courts are insisting that mentally handicapped people and their families have rights too." He shook his head and grinned. "I'm sorry, Mrs. Wadonelli. I sound like I need a soap box. What I mean by all of this is that by taking her out ... say, shopping, she has learned that she cannot pick something off the shelves and keep it. She has learned that it is stealing and stealing is wrong. She's tried it a few times and was punished for it. Now, she knows it is wrong. I'm not saying she wouldn't ever try it again if she were told to do it by other kids, however. I think, as far as Barry is concerned, all you can do is take him out with you just as much as possible and teach him the right things to do on the spot. At least, it's worked for us."

Joan nodded. "We probably haven't been taking him out in public enough. We will from now on. I feel that he didn't realize it was wrong."

The officer got up to leave. "I know you'll do the right thing, Mrs. Wadonelli. Just remember, these kids can be taken in. They're very naive ... very gullible. A lot of retarded girls get sexually assaulted because of this gullibility and trust." The officer chuckled to himself. "We once told Cindy to kill the light in the bedroom and she knocked it out with a broom handle. You have to be very careful with slang around them. They take everything literally."

Joan laughed in spite of the situation.

"Also, I'd keep Barry away from those Morton boys. I'm on my way out to meet with their folks." He turned and put out his hand. "Don't worry, Mrs. Wadonelli. I think you'll do fine with Barry."

Joan smiled as she held the door open for him. "I can promise you, we will surely try."

136

Chapter 15

Barry yawned and scratched his stomach as he came out of his bedroom in his pajamas. Pete lumbered in beside him, his claws clicking on the tile.

Barry pulled out the stool to the cupboard and climbed on it to reach Pete's bowl. He dumped in some dry, hard balls of dog food and poured milk over it and then placed it on the floor. Pete charged at it and ate hungrily.

Barry hummed as he busied himself around the kitchen. He put the tea kettle on the burner not bothering to turn it on, and placed two slices of bread in the toaster. He pulled a carton of butter and a jar of jam out of the refrigerator and started to place them on the table. They slipped out of his hands and fell to the floor spilling some of the contents. Next, he poured a large portion of dry cereal into two bowls and drenched them in milk. He ladled three heaping spoonfuls of coffee into each cup and poured the cold water from the kettle into them. Barry wrinkled his nose detecting a strange smell. He prodded his brain for information. Finally, he looked around discovering smoke billowing from the toaster. Climbing up on the stool once again, he released the toast so it popped up, revealing its burned state. Barry pulled the toast out, looked at it, and grimaced. Pete, having finished his meal, looked up and whimpered. Barry placed the two black pieces of toast on the table and smiled triumphantly. At last, breakfast was ready for Mama and Daddy Wadi.

Pete walked with Barry into Joan and Carl's bedroom. Barry opened the door carefully and peeked inside. The room was silent except for the heavy inhaling and exhaling of Carl's deep breathing. Barry grimaced and let out a shrieking warhoop, charging into the room bounding upon Carl's stomach. Pete ran excitedly to Joan's side of the bed and jumped up, licking her face. Carl reared up, gasping, trying to quickly orient himself while Joan batted at Pete's long, wet tongue.

"Mama and Daddy Wadi, come on; come!" shouted Barry.

Carl rubbed his eyes trying to persuade his brain to function on such short notice. Joan threw her dangling hair curlers at Pete.

"What time is it, anyway?" Carl asked disbelievingly.

Barry pulled Carl's hand. "Come on ... come on and see. Hurry!"

Carl got out of bed and shuffled, barefoot, into the kitchen like a stubborn dog on a leash. Joan scuffed in behind him executing a large, open-mouthed yawn.

"What in heaven's name?" She looked at her kitchen which had been left immaculate the night before. The floor was sticky with globs of jam. Black, crusty crumbs of toast lay about the table. Puddles of milk, looking like miniature lakes, were on the table and floor. Placing her hands on her hips, her temper started to flare. Then she looked at Barry's proud, pleased face. She looked at Pete whose tail was wagging like an out-of-control metronome.

Carl stood with a contented smile on his face. "Well, would you look at this, Joan? Isn't this something?" Carl asked grinning from ear to ear.

Joan nodded half-heartedly and forced herself to smile.

Barry pulled a chair out for Joan. "Mama Wadi, sit down and eat. I made it for you."

Joan sat down and looked at the disarray of barely edible items. "It ... it looks great, hon." Bringing the coffee to her lips, she choked as the cold, bitter mixture ran down her throat.

Barry watched her, perplexed.

Carl stirred the soggy cereal around in his bowl trying to evoke enough courage for the first bite.

"Eat some toast," Barry urged.

There was still a smoky haze in the air from the charred bread.

Joan smiled and spread butter and jam on the black toast. She bit into it and it crumbled in her hand. Meanwhile, Carl attempted his cold coffee.

Joan set her toast down and stared at it. "Oh, my, I guess I'm not as hungry as I thought."

"Me either," Carl said.

A disappointed frown came to Barry's face.

Joan winced and looked at Carl. He heaved a deep sigh of resignation.

"Well, I don't know, though, it does look good," he said. "You know, I think I could polish this off in nothing flat."

Joan rubbed the back of her neck peering down at the soggy cereal. "It does look tempting, especially this cereal." She poked a large spoonful into her mouth, held her breath and shuddered.

Barry looked up and smiled.

Carl crunched on his burned toast, one regretful bite after the other.

Barry propped his chin on top of his fists on the edge of the table. He watched his mom and dad consume each and every bite until the whole breakfast was gone.

Joan sighed as she managed to swallow the last of her coffee. Pulling Barry to her, she kissed his bald head. "That was very thoughtful of you."

"And Pete, too," Barry reminded her in a gutteral voice.

Joan looked at Carl and patted his hand. "You know, it's only a few days before Christmas. I've got to get going on things." She paused and looked at Barry. "How would you like Grandmama Wadonelli to come over for Christmas Eve?"

Barry's face lit up. "Yes! Yes! I like Grandma Wadi."

Carl chucked Joan under the chin affectionately. "That's real nice of you, Joan, especially the way she's acted lately."

They both looked at Barry who grimaced and stuck out his tongue.

"Well, Carl, it's Christmas, afterall. I thought I'd call her and see if she would come. Leona May said that she, Herbie, and the kids were going to his folks for the holidays. All the rest of your family live so far away. I don't want her to be alone on Christmas."

Carl nodded. "I haven't heard from her in weeks. Just a couple of phone calls and then she just said what she had to and hung up." He shook his head. "She's a stubborn woman."

"I know. But we haven't tried to 'mend fences' either. We've been so busy with our lives and with Barry, I'm afraid we've neglected her."

"She deserved a lot of it, Joan. Even if she is my Grandma and the woman who helped raise me."

"Yes, but she's a proud woman. I know, as you do, that down deep, she's good. You used to tell me all the time how strong she was when your parents were killed. And she did take care of you for over eight years."

Carl smiled in reflection. "Well, of course, I would like her here on Christmas Eve, but I'm going to leave it up to Barry. He's the one who deserves the apology."

Joan and Carl looked at Barry who was involved in petting Pete. He looked up.

"Do you want Grandmama Wadonelli to come over for Christmas Eve, Barry?" Joan asked.

Barry paused for a moment and then jumped up and down clapping his hands. "Yes, yes! I make Grandma Wadi a present at school."

Joan nodded and smiled. "Well, the decision's been made. I'll call her today."

A smile came to Carl's face. "Hey, how about putting up a real big tree this year? We always had one for Rick. Barry and I could go to that tree farm on the highway and cut one ... a real big one!"

Joan sat back in her chair and placed her hand beneath her chin. "That sounds nice. It's Barry's first Christmas with us and we want to make it special for him."

"Another thing is Christmas shopping." He looked down at

Barry and tapped him lightly on the head. "I don't know, Joan," he said teasingly, "do you think this kid has been good enough to deserve a present? Sometimes, he's been a real big pain in the neck, you know."

Joan looked at Carl and smiled in thought. "Yes, I know, and sometimes he's been a real good kid."

Their eyes met and instant tears of happiness formed. They both looked away in embarrassment.

Carl cleared his throat. "Well, I'll see what I can do about it."

Barry looked up at them, confused with the teasing and double meanings.

"Why don't I do the dishes and you two go outside and throw snow balls or make a fort or something. In short, get out of my kitchen so I can get some work done." Playfully, she shooed them away.

"You got yourself a deal," Carl said. "Come on, Barry, let's get dressed so we can go outside. I'm going to show you how to build the biggest, fattest snowman you ever saw."

"Fatter than you, Daddy Wadi?" Barry asked seriously.

Joan and Carl burst out laughing.

Joan watched out of the window as Carl and Barry rolled huge, packed balls of snow. In the distance she heard Barry's hoarse giggle as the snowman progressed from just a base to a torso and then to a head. Carl tackled Barry and would fling him down in the deep snow. Barry screamed with delight and begged for mercy.

Joan felt more at peace than she had since Ricky's death. What a change this little mentally handicapped boy had made in their lives, she thought. And now there was an added blessing that she hadn't told Carl about. She vowed to surprise him on Christmas Eve. She found out just days ago that she was pregnant. She had a good feeling about it this time. She knew it would go full term. Everything seemed normal. God did allow her another miracle just like Father Shawn said He would. Barry would one day have a little brother or sister.

She watched Carl lift Barry up to implant a potato in the snowman's face. Barry shouted with excitement as they finished the face of the snowman.

Pete was friskier than he had been in months. Last winter, he had to be shoved out the door twice a day for exercise and to relieve himself. This winter, whenever Barry put on his coat, Pete was immediately at his side, his tail wagging out of control.

Joan pushed back the curtain watching them as they pulled an old red stocking cap over the snowman's head and encircled its neck with a scarf. Barry continued packing more snow around the snowman's middle.

At last, the two of them backed away and took a long, gratified look at their creation. The snowman was finished and stood guard at the entrance of their yard.

Suddenly, they turned and raced to the house. Sounds of stomping boots, laughter, and screams exploded through the door. Joan stood ready to accept wet coats, gloves, and socks. She had mugs of piping hot cocoa waiting.

Carl walked to the window and looked out. He motioned for Joan to join him. His face was glowing from the bitter cold. "What do you think, Joan? Does it or doesn't it look like me?"

Joan pretended that her reply was of utmost importance. She squinted into the sunlight and surveyed the creation like an artist judging a rare work of sculpture. Finally, she cupped her chin in deliberation. "I think it looks very much like the model except it could use a whole lot more snow on the stomach."

Carl gave her a playful nudge and laughed. Barry laughed, too, even though the joke had escaped him.

"That's Daddy Wadi." He pointed to the snowman. "It looks like him." Barry rubbed his own stomach. "He's real big here like Daddy Wadi and ..." He paused to think of the right words. " ... and here." He placed his fist on his nose.

Carl looked around and frowned. "Does he always have to be so darned honest?"

Joan laughed while Carl rolled Barry over and over on the rug feigning revenge for the insult he had just given.

At last, the three of them sat down to their cocoa. Barry wiggled his bare toes in the nap of the carpet. Carl lay back in his easy chair, his eyes closed. Barry sat scratching Pete's long, limp ears as he slept.

Suddenly, Barry bolted to the window and looked out. Pete jumped up, startled out of his deep sleep. Barry screamed an inarticulate phrase and ran out the door and down the porch steps.

Joan looked at Carl, completely confused. She ran to the window to look out, and saw the Morton boys in the yard in the process of demolishing the snowman. They kicked it and pushed at the huge balls of snow to topple it.

"My god, Carl," she yelled, "Barry's barefoot! He'll catch pneumonia. Stop him!"

Both of them arrived at the door in time to see Barry positioned on top of Mick Morton punching him with clenched fists. Donny Morton was almost out of sight running down the graveled road trying to escape.

"Stop him, Carl! He'll catch cold out there and besides it looks like he's ready to kill that Morton kid!"

A slow, flushed smile of pride crept into Carl's face. He heard what those boys put Barry up to a couple of weeks ago. He remembered how Dusty ridiculed and demeaned Barry and he smiled. "Yeah, he's taking care of that little smart aleck, isn't he?"

Mick Morton squirmed with fright, his arms flailing in every direction as Barry held him down in the snow.

"Carl, go out there and stop it!" Joan screamed.

"Yeah, yeah, I will, I will ... in a minute." Carl slowly moved toward the door.

Barry's fist caught Mick on the nose and a stream of blood oozed from his nostrils. A wail of agony cut through the quiet winter morning.

Barry slowly got to his feet. Mick jumped up and ran down the road bawling for his mother, yelling every four letter word he knew, and holding a handkerchief to his bleeding nose.

Joan was frantic with concern while Carl was taking the whole incident with remarkable calm.

Barry trudged slowly up the steps and into the house. He started to shiver. Joan ran to him and started kneading his bare feet. "I know you'll get pneumonia from this. What in the world got into you to do such a thing?" she asked. "A snowman isn't worth catching your death over."

Barry looked up at her. "It was Daddy Wadi ... he was knocking down the snowman like Daddy Wadi."

"I don't care who it was. You're going to have a hot bath, young man, and then crawl right into bed," she admonished.

Carl looked down at Barry as Joan fawned over him. He smiled and winked at his son.

Barry looked up at his father and smiled.

Chapter 16

Mama pulled the turkey from the oven and the aroma wafted through the small house, tantalizing her tastebuds. She pulled her shawl up around her shoulders and poked the turkey critically with a fork, satisfied that it was progressing according to plan. With a satisfied nod, she shoved it back to bake longer. Mama took her hanky from her tight sleeve and wiped between her first and second chins.

"Anything that I cannot stand is dry turkey," she said wrinkling her forehead. "I always serve it with its natural juices still oozing out of it. My sister, Marisa, is known for her dry turkey. Fifteen years ago Christmas Day, Martino, Carl's second cousin, choked on her dry meat." Mama clutched at her throat in pantomime. "Sweet Jesus, his face turned every shade of purple. Luigi nearly had his arm, up to his elbow, down Martino's throat before he pulled the glob out. God in Heaven," she crossed herself, "I thought we were going to lose him. Ever since that day I have been sure I baste it continuously to preserve its moisture." Mama ran a thumb under her tight corset. She was packed as tight as a sausage in a black, silk casing. A waxed poinsettia rested between the huge mounds of her breasts.

Joan hummed a Christmas carol under her breath as she pulled apart a crisp head of lettuce for a salad. She had her back turned to Mama as she worked.

Mama placed her hands on her broad hips and licked her upper lip with agitation.

"It looks like Mama is talking to herself. Mama's stories of the family doesn't seem to be worth noting by my Carl's wife," she said with an irritating edge in her voice.

Joan looked over her shoulder. "Did you say something, Mama?"

Mama shrugged her round shoulders and pulled at her shawl. She raised her hands to the heavens. "I don't know, Papa. No one listens to or respects Mama anymore. Perhaps, it's time Mama joined you. I seem just to be excess baggage these days. I suppose Mama has outlived her usefulness." She crossed herself and wilted into a chair, dejected.

Such self-pity used to infuriate Joan, but lately she felt that she understood that Mama Wadonelli was fighting old age, insecurity, and loneliness. She really was a very frightened woman. The family did not depend upon her any more as it once did.

Joan smiled and walked over to her and pecked her fat cheek. "I'm sorry, Mama. I was just thinking how happy I am."

Mama nodded and wiped her upper lip with her hanky and then dabbed at her eyes. "It seems to me this would be the saddest Christmas you've ever had. This is the first year your precious child, God's perfect angel, is not with you and Carl."

Joan nodded and then shrugged. "Of course, we miss Ricky. There's not a day we don't think about him. But, Carl and I are the happiest we've been in many months." She looked at Mama. "You know what it is, don't you, Mama?"

"Mama would have to be pretty dull-witted not to understand. Give Mama credit for something."

Joan smiled. "Ever since Barry came to live with us, life has been different. I don't know how to explain it." She thought for a moment. "It's been so full and rewarding. Just like Mrs. Bertrand said it would be, months ago, with Amy."

Mama looked up, her thick eyebrows furrowed.

"Oh, it's a long story, Mama. You don't want to hear it." Joan waved her hand and returned to the salad.

Mama looked toward heaven and mumbled about not being informed by anyone these days.

Suddenly, Joan gasped with excitement. "They're coming with the tree, Mama! They're coming with the tree!"

Mama shrugged and pulled at her shawl. "So, they're coming with the tree. It's just a tree, nothing special." She shrugged again. "I still think a good aluminum tree is best. You just pull it out of the closet and snap the branches on it every year. And then the day after Christmas pull it apart and put it in the closet. There's no expense and no danger of fire. And you don't have to spend a whole day pulling pine needles out of the carpet."

"I know you have one of those. But, this Christmas is Barry's first with us and we wanted to make it special. We wanted to have a real tree just like when Ricky was with us."

Mama pulled at her shawl and shrugged. "To each his own. Live and let live, I always say."

Carl and Barry stomped their boots on the porch. They charged through the door dragging an ideally formed eight foot Scotch pine behind them. Barry's bald head was covered with a bright green stocking cap. His face was flushed from the excitement and the biting cold. Mucous ran in twin streams under his nose with unconcern. An upturned tongue now and then prohibited its running uncontained. A matching green scarf encircled his neck. Carl pulled his stocking cap off and began unbuttoning his mackinaw. Barry pulled off his cap and slowly began to unbutton his coat one button at a time with his tongue hanging out of the corner of his mouth as he concentrated on the task.

Joan gathered up coats and hats to take them to the closet. Mama waddled into the livingroom, gathering her shawl around her with a scowl on her face.

"Close the door, Carl! The snow is blowing in. Haven't you two any concern for other people?" Mama scolded.

Barry looked up at her, grimacing and stuck out his cracked tongue. Mama turned her head away and shuddered.

"Mama," Carl said, "I feel so warm inside, I can't imagine anyone being cold."

Mama glanced at Barry out of the corner of her eye. "I don't know what you are talking about."

Joan re-entered the room and looked at the tree resting on the carpet.

"You're going to be picking pine needles out of the nap until Easter," Mama warned.

"A few pine needles won't hurt anybody," Carl stated.

"Hold it up by the tip," Joan instructed.

Barry raced to get the stool. He stood on top of it, holding the tree straight. Joan walked around it, praising its height, color, and form. Barry beamed with pride.

"Daddy Wadi and me drove clear out," he pointed with his finger, "and we cut it ourselves. Only two bucks a foot!" Barry shouted.

Mama shook her head. "Such expense ... such waste." She made clucking noises with her tongue.

Carl patted Barry on the back. "Go over there and give your Grandmama a kiss, Barry."

Barry ran to Mama. He stood there looking up at her, his lips pursed.

Mama peered at him with her little pig eyes and winced. Reluctantly, she bent forward and Barry encircled her neck and kissed her hard on her third chin.

Mama sat back rigid and frowned. "Next time you want him to kiss Mama, wipe his runny nose. Mama can feel snot on her face."

Barry looked up, grimaced, and stuck out his tongue.

She bowed her head and made the sign of the cross. "Jesus, give Mama strength."

Joan ran to Barry and handed him a handkerchief. "Blow your nose, Barry, and then help your dad put the tree in the stand while Grandmama and I see about getting things ready to eat."

After supper, Mama sat in a large overstuffed chair with a pout on her bloated face. She watched Carl, Joan, and Barry trim the tree. She could not reconcile herself to them having this child whose eyes did not follow his head. This child, who did not know the Catholic Prayer of Contrition, or the Pennitential Rite, or the Profession of Faith or any of the proper Catholic prayers. Did he even know the Lord or His Mother, Mary? She doubted it. He hardly knew anything. She rolled her eyes back in disgust as he dropped a glass ornament and it shattered on the floor.

"The boy has too many bulbs on that one branch. It's weighing it down," Mama criticized.

Joan climbed down off the step stool and cocked her head from one side to the other, appraising the tree.

"I think Mama's right, Barry," Joan said. "Take a couple of them off and hang them on a lower branch."

Barry nodded and did as he was told without comment.

Carl put on a record of Christmas carols and its sound filled the house. Pete howled when some of the notes hit a pitch that hurt his ears. Barry threw his arms around him and give him a hug at every opportunity and Pete lapped his face gratefully.

Finally, Joan took Barry by the hand. "Come on, Carl, step back and look at it. Isn't it great? Doesn't it send chills down your spine?"

Carl stepped back with his wife and son surveying the tree critically. "I'd say it was the best looking tree in town." He nudged Barry with an elbow. "How about you?"

Barry looked up. He pointed to the top of the tree. "Daddy Wadi, it needs an angel."

Joan chuckled. "Oh, of course it does! Barry, why don't you go get it in the box and Dad will lift you up to put it on the top branch."

Barry dipped his hand down into the box of odds and ends of Christmas ornaments and finally pulled out an old tattered cardboard angel holding a plastic candle with a miniature light bulb. Straggly tufts of cotton, representing hair, hung pitifully down the angel's shoulders.

Barry held it up proudly and smiled.

An audible "Ugh!" came from Mama.

Carl hoisted Barry to his shoulders. Barry strained until his face turned red as he set the angel on the topmost branch. He shoved it down over the limb and it stood there leaning to one side. He turned and grinned proudly.

Joan started to get the stool to straighten the angel, but

stopped when she looked at Barry's beaming face.

Mama pointed at the angel, shaking her head with annoyance.

Carl kissed Barry's head. "Now, that's what I call a tree! Barry, you go over and plug the lights in and let's see what she looks like."

Barry looked up at Carl, confused as to what he was supposed to do.

Carl nodded toward the nearest plug in.

Mama made the sign of the cross praying that he wouldn't blow up the entire living room. Joan switched off the lights and waited eagerly. Suddenly, the entire tree lit up in one glorious blaze of color and lights except for the bulb of the lopsided angel which remained dark.

Barry clapped his hands with joy at the spectacle. Joan sniffled in her handkerchief, overcome, as she lay her head on Carl's shoulder. In the background, Bing Crosby sang a medley of Christmas songs.

Barry ran to Mama and grabbed her pudgy hand. "Come on Grandma Wadi, let's sing Christmas songs! Please, Grandma, sing with us."

Mama stood her ground, refusing to budge. "No! No … Mama just wants to watch. Leave Mama alone, child. No one wants Mama around these days."

Barry grimaced. "I want you to sing with us. Please, Grandma." He tugged at her hand with determination.

Mama threw her hands up. "Oh, why can't everyone leave Mama alone! Mama cannot sing!"

"Sing about Jesus, Grandma," Barry pleaded.

Mama frowned. "What do you know about Jesus? You don't know about Him. The Son of our Father."

"I know about Him, Grandma. I learned about Him in religion class."

Mama raised a dark eyebrow with skepticism. "Oh, you did. What can a boy like you know and understand about our Saviour? Don't tell me you know about Him. He knows everything about everybody. He never errs. Don't tell me that you know anything about Him. He made you."

Joan started to interrupt in Barry's defense. Carl pulled her back before she had a chance to speak.

"Don't tell me you know anything," Mama continued. "You are not all there. How can you know?"

Barry looked at her and scrunched up his face. "My teacher said I was retarded." He thought for a moment. "But, she said it was all right because I'm the way I'm supposed to be." He grimaced and thought again. "Because God never makes mistakes. That's why you're supposed to love everybody just the way they are."

Mama looked down at Barry's flat, round face and said nothing. She looked up at Carl and Joan and then back to Barry. A muscle flexed under one eye. A tear slowly seeped out of a corner of her eye and ran down the mounds of her cheeks. She started to speak and her voice broke. She cleared her throat and then continued. "Mama is ashamed. I thought I knew God. For years I have been praying to the Father and expecting everyone to believe because I wanted it. I demanded it. Yet, I have been wrong so many times." Mama looked again at Barry. "And it took a child's innocence to show me how wrong I have been." She looked at Carl and Joan, her eyes filled with tears. This time there was no exhibition of emotion. "What Mama has done to you and this sweet child is unforgivable. Perhaps ... perhaps in your hearts, since it is Christmas, you can forgive a very foolish old woman." She looked with sad eyes at Carl. "Carl?"

Carl smiled and nodded.

"Joan?"

Joan went to her and pulled her close. Mama bucked up and down in sorrow and relief. Joan released her finally and Mama embraced Barry pulling him into her huge bosoms. Barry turned his head away after a few moments gasping for breath. She kissed his cheek.

"Look at Mama. A little child has taught me the meaning of being a true Christian. Thank God you came into my life before it was too late! I never wanted to listen to anyone. Mama knew everything. It was you, Joan, and my grandson, Carl," she nodded toward them, "… and your little son, Barry, who invited Mama for Christmas while the rest of the family shunned me." She sobbed into her hanky with remorse. "And the way Mama treated you. Yet, it was you who thought of Mama this Christmas." She cried openly, all of her chins vibrating under the onslaught of grief and shame. "Papa, in Heaven, must be so ashamed of me. The way I've treated Leona May's husband, Herbert, who is a good man even though he doesn't attend any church and never will because of me." Mama looked up, her lower lip quivering. "And I've asked God for another miracle for you. That you would one day have a child as perfect as Ricky. Why should God grant me anything the way I've been?"

Joan couldn't help smiling to herself.

Mama blew her nose with a loud honk. "I beg forgiveness from all of you. If you don't grant it, I will understand. I did nothing but ridicule Barry and everything he did, even the way he put up that angel … all lopsided." Mama broke down once more.

Carl walked over to her and placed his arm around her stout shoulders. "Mama, come! Let's sing carols with the record. Bing is about ready to go into 'The First Noel'. Please, Mama, we understand."

Mama dabbed at her eyes and walked slowly toward the tree all alight except for the angel on top. Mama started singing with Bing Crosby but broke down intermittently into loud sobs. Carl and Joan's voices rang out boldly. Barry tried to follow along but kept looking up at Mama sobbing in her handkerchief. He was totally confused.

As the hymn ended, Carl turned the record player off and it spun to an out-of-focus groan and finally stopped.

"Now, everybody, what say we open our presents?" Carl cried.

Barry jumped straight up with excitement.

Joan's eyes glittered with pleasure and anticipation. "Yes, that's a good idea! Let Barry open his first before he turns himself inside out," Joan said.

Barry jumped up and down, clapping his hands.

Carl reached for a long, slender package under the tree. He handed it to Barry. "Merry Christmas, son."

Joan placed her arm around Carl's waist as they watched Barry slowly try to figure how to untie the ribbon. Finally, he could stand it no longer and ripped the wrapping without concern. He pulled out a new rod and reel ready for assembly.

"It's for those big ones we're going to catch at Neosha Lake one of these days," Carl said, smiling.

Presents were passed back and forth with everyone thanking everyone else for their thoughtfulness and choice of gifts. Mama finally pulled herself together and was rattling half-English, half-Italian phrases, hands flying. The tree looked like a green island surrounded by a sea of bright paper and ribbon. Barry suddenly started to dig beneath the paper and ribbon frantically.

"What's the matter, hon? What is it?" Joan asked.

Barry looked up. "Where is Grandma Wadi's? I wrapped it at school. Mrs. Pinkerton helped me."

Carl moved through the debris like a human bulldozer searching for the gift. Finally, a little red package tied with green ribbon was found among the discarded paper.

Barry handed the package to Mama. He beamed with pride. "I made it for you at school."

Mama accepted it and tried to control her trembling fingers as she unwrapped the package. "Not one of my greatgrand babies gave Mama a gift ... not one. You are the only one." She untied the ribbon and unwrapped the gift. Nestled in an overuse of paper was a little match stick crib occupied by a papier-mache baby.

Barry grimaced and announced in his gravel voice, "That's baby Jesus in his bed."

Mama looked up at the smiling faces of Carl and Joan. The same muscle began to flex beneath her eye and her chins started to vibrate like a volcano preparing to erupt. She pulled Barry to her and held him for several moments. "It's the finest gift Mama has ever received, my little bambino. Thank you so much for remembering."

Joan brushed a tear from her eye as Carl pressed a finger beneath his nose straining for composure.

At last, Joan went to Barry and pulled him from Mama's grasp. "It's time for bed, Barry."

Barry looked at his new rod and reel and started to protest until he caught Joan's stern warning.

"We'll put it all together in the morning, son," Carl assured him.

Barry received a hug from Mama, Carl, and Joan and then turned toward his room. He turned around just before he entered. "Merry Christmas!" he said. He opened his bedroom door and closed it behind him.

Joan looked out of her bedroom window at the sun reflecting off the virgin snow. Fresh snow had fallen during the night and lay like a white blanket without a track of human existence to mar its perfection. She lay there for a moment and stretched like a contented cat. The world seemed full of joy and love this morning, she thought as she looked out at the new day. Even Mama had relented to Barry's charms. Everyone was a better person since Barry had come into their lives, she thought. She told only Carl about her pregnancy last night when they got ready for bed. He broke down and cried with happiness. She decided to wait for awhile before telling Mama.

Turning, she looked at Carl sleeping. He breathed in and then expelled the air through his mouth, making a sound much like air escaping a tire valve. She watched his stomach rise and fall in a relaxed, contented rhythm. They had never been closer, she thought. She could hardly believe that in just a few months that Barry had been with them how much better everything was.

Carl grunted in his sleep and turned to his side. The bed moaned under the shift of his weight. Joan rocked about as if she were in a rowboat hit by a strong wind. Months ago, things like that irritated her, but lately she found it comforting to have him lying at her side. Leaning over, she nibbled his ear. He muttered under his breath and hit at the air.

Joan felt mischievous on this glorious Christmas day. She pulled a thread off her nightgown and tickled his large nose. Carl grunted with gutteral, unconscious protests until he at last raised up, flailing the air. Joan giggled. Carl realized he had been duped and started tickling her. She laughed, trying to move away from him.

"Carl, stop it!"

He ignored her pleas.

"Hon, you're going to wake Mama and Barry. They need their sleep after all of the excitement last night."

At last Carl relented and allowed her to get out of bed and slip on a robe.

He lifted the alarm clock on the night stand and squinted at its fluorescent numerals. "It's going on eight o'clock. I thought that little pistol would be up at the crack of dawn he'd be so excited about his new rod and reel."

Joan looked down at Carl, smiling.

"What is it, Joan? Why're you grinning?" he asked.

"Oh, I just feel good. You know, it being Barry's first Christmas and the excitement and expectation of the new baby and all." She thought for a moment. "And Mama getting so close to Barry. And her accepting Herbie as a true member of this family. Everything is falling into place this Christmas."

Carl looked up at the ceiling in contemplation. "You're right. Barry has changed us all. He has a gift, that's for sure. We're going to have years and years of great Christmases with him and the new one." Carl slipped into deep thought for a moment. "You know, Joan, like I told you, I'm going to have Barry help me with the spring planting. That'll be good for him."

Joan nodded her agreement.

Carl patted his stomach that rose beneath the blanket. "Boy, I'm getting hungry. Let's go in and wake Barry and make some breakfast so he and I can eat and get started putting that rod and reel together."

"You're always hungry," Joan said, playfully poking his stomach. She scooted her feet into her slippers. "I can't understand why he isn't up." She extended her hand and pulled with all her strength to help Carl out of bed.

Opening Barry's door carefully, Joan peered inside. The room was dark because of the drawn shades. Joan tiptoed over to Barry's bed with Carl close behind. She cautioned him with a finger at her lips. She switched on the table lamp next to his bed. The light illumined his face and Toto resting on the pillow beside him.

Joan bent down to kiss him on the cheek and to wish him a merry Christmas. Carl waited his turn to grab him by the heels and stand him on end. He wanted to hear his graveled voice beg happily for mercy.

Joan reared back as though she had been stung. She looked down at him. "My god, Carl, he's so cold."

Carl moved Joan out of the way and grabbed Barry's hand. It was hard and waxy. He placed his ear on Barry's chest. Carl lifted Barry to a sitting position and gasped as his head fell backwards without support. Pete placed his front paws on the bed and started to whimper.

Carl looked at Joan in disbelief. "He's gone, Joan. Barry is gone."

Joan clutched her mouth as though she was going to be sick. "Oh, god, no. No!"

Carl tucked the blankets around him as though he were trying to make him comfortable. Finally, he stepped back and looked at Joan. The tears streamed from his eyes.

Joan made a strained, choking sound, trying to reach for Barry, yet not touching him with her trembling hands. "Why, Carl? Why did he die?" He was so happy last night. This was going to be his first Christmas with us." She fell into Carl's arms, sobbing out of control.

Carl held her close as she convulsed in anguish.

"I don't suppose anybody knows. Remember, Mrs. Bertrand said kids like Barry are susceptible to all kinds of illnesses. It could've been his heart. It looks like it just gave out and he went peacefully. The blankets aren't even mussed. He went real easy, Joan."

"I don't want to go on without him." She choked and then wept openly.

"Maybe he did what he was supposed to do here on earth. He came into our lives when we were sad and desperate and he stayed until the miracle happened. He showed people how they should get along with each other. Maybe he did what he was supposed to do and then he was called to Heaven." Carl shook his head. "I don't know, Joan. I just don't know."

Joan knelt down and kissed Barry. This time, he did not smile or grimace. "Oh, god," she said, "I miss him already."

"I'd better call someone, Joan. We need to call Father Shawn so he can give him the Last Rite." He thought for a moment. "And then the county coroner, I guess, to report his death." Carl walked into the living room and picked up the phone.

"Wait!" Joan said. "Don't call just yet. Please give me a little time with him before they take him away."

Carl started to protest but placed the phone back on the hook after looking at her pleading eyes. "Sure, hon, take all the time you need."

Together, they walked to the divan. Pete came to them whimpering, sensing that something tragic had taken place with his good friend.

Carl looked at the package holding the rod and reel they were planning to assemble this morning. "He would've gotten a real kick out of Lake Neosha. There's nothing like getting up early in the morning at the crack of dawn and fishing in the chilly morning air. Makes you feel like a real man." His voice broke. Carl's eye caught the picture setting on the coffee table of Barry and him at the park lake. Barry was holding up the little sun perch beaming with pride. Tears raced down his cheeks as he thought of that day, that wonderful day, when he first realized he wanted Barry for his son.

Joan's glazed eyes looked at the wrappings around the tree.

She thought about last night and the laughter and joy they had trimming the tree. She looked at the tree with its decorations placed on it with care. She smiled in spite of her sorrow remembering Carl hoisting Barry on his shoulders to place the tattered angel on the top of the tree. There it stood lopsided with its bulb that refused to light.

"Plug in the lights, Carl," Joan said, wiping her eyes. "Barry was so proud of that tree. He thought he did such a good job decorating."

Carl gave her a quick embrace and got to his feet. He blew his nose and then leaned over and plugged in the Christmas lights. Immediately, the tree took on a spectacular brilliance as every light popped on. Carl's and Joan's eyes trailed up the tree to the lopsided angel whose bulb flickered for a moment and then lighted.

The End